"*Pink* wraps what has been and what is into a unique and compelling story of what will be. Jennifer Harris grounds the reader with her in both time and place presenting a read that is, at one moment in time, poetic, fantastic, and fun. In *Pink,* Ms. Harris engages the reader at every level through the 'what ifs' of her own life by delving into her own psyche and relationships with family and lovers, keeping the reader turning the page late into the night.

I found Ms. Harris's use of the future to tell a self-investigation of the now, a unique device that not only worked but allowed more inward challenges for both author and reader by not divulging (or clearly defining for the reader) that line between what is the then and what is the now and what is the was. A true poetic read."

—Raymond Hammond
Editor, *New York Quarterly*
poetry magazine

NOTES FOR PROFESSIONAL LIBRARIANS AND LIBRARY USERS

This is an original book title published by Alice Street Editions™, Harrington Park Press®, the Trade Division of The Haworth Press, Inc. Unless otherwise noted in specific chapters with attribution, materials in this book have not been previously published elsewhere in any format or language.

CONSERVATION AND PRESERVATION NOTES

All books published by The Haworth Press, Inc., and its imprints are printed on certified pH neutral, acid-free book grade paper. This paper meets the minimum requirements of American National Standard for Information Sciences-Permanence of Paper for Printed Material, ANSI Z39.48-1984.

DIGITAL OBJECT IDENTIFIER (DOI) LINKING

The Haworth Press is participating in reference linking for elements of our original books. (For more information on reference linking initiatives, please consult the CrossRef Web site at www.crossref.org.) When citing an element of this book such as a chapter, include the element's Digital Object Identifier (DOI) as the last item of the reference. A Digital Object Identifier is a persistent, authoritative, and unique identifier that a publisher assigns to each element of a book. Because of its persistence, DOIs will enable The Haworth Press and other publishers to link to the element referenced, and the link will not break over time. This will be a great resource in scholarly research.

Pink

Pink

Jennifer Harris

Alice Street Editions™
Harrington Park Press®
The Trade Division of The Haworth Press, Inc.
New York • London • Oxford

For more information on this book or to order, visit
http://www.haworthpress.com/store/product.asp?sku=5768

or call 1-800-HAWORTH (800-429-6784) in the United States and Canada
or (607) 722-5857 outside the United States and Canada

or contact orders@HaworthPress.com

Published by

Alice Street Editions™, Harrington Park Press®, the trade division of The Haworth Press, Inc.,
10 Alice Street, Binghamton, NY 13904-1580.

PUBLISHER'S NOTE
The development, preparation, and publication of this work has been undertaken with great care.
However, the Publisher, employees, editors, and agents of The Haworth Press are not responsible
for any errors contained herein or for consequences that may ensue from use of materials or information contained in this work. The Haworth Press is committed to the dissemination of ideas and
information according to the highest standards of intellectual freedom and the free exchange of
ideas. Statements made and opinions expressed in this publication do not necessarily reflect the
views of the Publisher, Directors, management, or staff of The Haworth Press, Inc., or an
endorsement by them.

This is a work of fiction. Names, characters, places, and incidents either are the products of the
author's imagination or are used fictitiously, and any resemblance to actual persons, living or
dead, business establishments, events, or locales is entirely coincidental.

Cover design by Lora Wiggins.
Cover illustration by Laurenn McCubbin.

Library of Congress Cataloging-in-Publication Data

Harris, Jennifer, 1969-
    Pink / Jennifer Harris.
        p. cm.
    ISBN-13: 978-1-56023-629-0 (soft : alk. paper)
    ISBN-10: 1-56023-629-9 (soft : alk. paper)
        1. Lesbian authors—Illinois—Chicago-Fiction. 2. Chicago (Ill.)—
Fiction. I. Title.

PS3558.A6424P56 2007
813'.6—dc22

                                                                    2006029408

To Susan Griffith.
Thank you for loving me so well.

Editor's Foreword

Alice Street Editions provides a voice for established as well as upcoming lesbian writers, reflecting the diversity of lesbian interests, ethnicities, ages, and class. This cutting-edge series of novels, memoirs, and nonfiction writing welcomes the opportunity to present controversial views, explore multicultural ideas, encourage debate, and inspire creativity from a variety of lesbian perspectives. Through enlightening, illuminating, and provocative writing, Alice Street Editions can make a significant contribution to the visibility and accessibility of lesbian writing and bring lesbian-focused writing to a wider audience. Recognizing our own desires and ideas in print is life sustaining, acknowledging the reality of who we are, as well as our place in the world, individually and collectively.

Judith P. Stelboum
Editor in Chief
Alice Street Editions

Acknowledgments

I would like to thank my parents for their continued love and support. You've always been there for me and I am so grateful.

I also must truly thank Dr. Judith Stelboum and everyone at Haworth, especially Tara Davis. Thank you, thank you, thank you. . . .

ONE

Every time I go into a bookstore I want to vomit. It usually starts in the G section of fiction but it's in full swing by the time I reach the Os. It's the type of feeling you get after eating too much ice cream. It hits you between the lungs, at the base near the gut. By the Os I want to shout: Hey, you forgot me! I look around, but all that I see is the book I will write. I can see the camera-ready art and everything. A slick title that will sell a million copies. It'll be me they're talking about on the news. They just don't know it yet.

The book I will write will make men sigh and bring tears like the best movie, the one you've seen a million times and can recite nearly by heart. My book will become a substitute for friends. It will be so sad that people won't want to finish, but they will skip to the back of the book to see if what they think will happen does, but it won't. My book will have a pink cover like the brightest cotton candy you loved as a kid so that every time you look at it you think of Ferris wheels. And there will be a gaudy display in the stores that I will tell everyone I hate, but that I will secretly love.

There will be a picture of the main character, me, standing in the middle of the desert. Low clouds will swirl behind me, in sandlike patterns, like at the beach when the waves retreat back into the ocean and the sand is all bumpy and streaked with imprints of the waves. That's how the clouds will be above me. And the title will be a thick black stripe across the top. But my name won't be on the front cover, only on the side because, aesthetically, I want the one-liner title and the picture. It will give you the feeling you had when your fifth grade teacher used your paper as the perfect example in class, even though you laughed, you will agree that somehow you are better than the rest.

My book will not have anything to do with self-help, self-love, or self-discovery, though it will lie next to those books on the shelf. When you enter the bookstore, you will hear people whispering what a great gift my book makes. The Pattersons will give it to the Thompsons and the Suttons will buy it for the Bradfords, who actu-

Pink
© 2007 by The Haworth Press, Inc. All rights reserved.
doi:10.1300/5768_01

ally already had it, so the Bradfords will give it to the Bickfords and it will be the most talked about book on the Internet. In fact, passages of it (even though it will infringe copyright laws) will be passed around in e-mails, traveling tens of thousands of miles a second, to over 60,000 nine-to-fivers in one day.

In a week my book will be quoted like everything in it was cliché, because in a week's time everyone will have heard about it and thought it was written way back, like before computers. When the sales clerk in Borders bookstore overhears people talking about it over coffee she will tell them it's sold out at the moment, but that a new shipment will be arriving shortly. Or if they want, she can call another store to see if they have it in stock, but the other store won't. The people having coffee will look at one another and pretend they've already read it. But they wouldn't have. They'll just want to. So they'll drink their lattes and look at the sales clerk and tell her thank you very much but that her help isn't necessary.

The pink of the cover of my book will catch everyone's eyes and hold them. The publisher will call me and ask if I want to go to California because a movie studio has decided my book will make a perfect film. Not movie or flick, but *film*. And not shot in video either. I will tell the publisher that I am trying to rest a little and that I will consider the offer, but that I'll need time to myself. After all, my book will be number one on *The New York Times* best seller list. I'll need time to bask. At least for a week or so. So I will hang up the phone and order Chinese.

My book will be shoved in between a pile of old copies of the manuscript, in my front hall closet, that will seem to be cleverly out of view, but if anyone comes over and hangs up their jacket they'll be sure to see it. It's like a condom in a guy's wallet. And I will consider whom I would like to see play myself as the lead. Though certainly it will depend on who's directing. Of course Woody Allen would be the natural choice if it was a comedy, but it's not. If I got what's his name, the *Platoon* guy, well, I'd have a paranoid version of my book, so maybe I'd choose the biggest of them all—Spielberg—even though I'd secretly be rooting for a French version so that everyone can die.

But that might be too close to the truth. Spielberg, on the other hand, could do wonders with my little pink book.

My little pink book will cause a fashion trend in Europe the likes of which hasn't been seen since Coco Chanel came on the scene. There will be book-shaped hats of bright pink in shimmery material so that the hat is as slick as the cover of my book, and there will be matching shoes with an ever-so-slight heel, enough to make a woman's calf look sexy but still low enough to be comfortable. After all, my book is intelligent.

The first time a reporter calls my apartment in Chicago I will have a mouthful of food and will have to excuse myself to spit it out. She will be from *The New Yorker* and I will say how sorry I am in a terribly charming way and she will laugh and apologize for catching me off guard and then write an article about how really sincere I am, about how shocking it is that I'm so simple while my writing is so insightful. She will ask how I can see through people that way. Do I believe in reincarnation? I will suggest we meet for lunch. But not anywhere fancy. It will be a family-style diner, the kind with fake plastic seats, where everything tastes like meat and potatoes, even the milkshakes. And I will warn her not to get a milkshake because of that. After she's gone, she will call and leave a message. "Can we meet? I think I have a few more questions. What about dinner?"

I will twirl a piece of bright pink ribbon in my hands, feeling the silk of it against my thumb, and I will consider the reporter. Consider a dinner. Would this be a date?

When I first get the acceptance letter from the publisher about the book I will write, I will walk inside my apartment and call my parents who will be as dumbstruck as me. We will laugh because it's the only thing we can think to do, like when someone dies and you lose your senses for an instant and you're trying to gather your thoughts, only it's so jumbled up you end up reacting in a way that's totally inappropriate. That is how it will be. My parents won't say anything at all. So I will hang up the phone, turn off the ringer, and cry. I mean pour-my-eyes-out cry, so hard that my stomach will contract and pull and hurt like someone's punched me because I will be suddenly terrified. I will feel all the blood rush in my veins, the way I do during a horror show, which is precisely why I won't go see horror shows. But I will feel the same way. That slowed-down feel. So slow you think you can see the sun inching down beneath the horizon. That scared feeling will stick with me for days. I will talk about the book a lot because I will be trying to talk all the fear out of me. But it won't work.

I will think that I made a terrible mistake. Maybe I should call up to New York, my editors, and tell them that the book needs a lot of work, that it's not ready. I will think that I need to put a stop to it. It can be better. I will swear. I will try to find some means of control but there won't be any. It will be sitting on a desk halfway across the country, being discussed and evaluated by a group of eleven executives. It will be out of my hands, so I will stock up my refrigerator and let all the food go bad. At first I'll think I'm going to eat it, but I will have lost my appetite, so I end up staring at the inside of the refrigerator for long stints of time, wondering if everyone who reads my book is going to hate it. I will think about taking a razor to my arms and slicing myself until they bleed. I will crave that sense of relief. I will imagine the blood falling out of me and each drop that leaves me makes me feel slightly better. But I won't have the nerve to pick up that blade.

When my little pink book is finally sitting on shelves in bookstores around the world, I will dance in my tiny apartment with all the windows wide open. I will turn on my favorite music, Nina Simone, and twirl around my apartment, letting my hips direct me. I will put my arms in the air up above my head and dance in slow circles. I will let the sound of her voice fill the room and me, and I will dance until I have to flip the record. I will dance all the way through side B too. And when I am feeling reckless, I will play The Beatles and jump up and down. John Lennon will sing to me, and I will think of all the dead people that have been and all the dead people to come. So I will turn up the volume and dance some more.

When I get tired, I will collapse on my hardwood floors and I will stare up at my cracked ceiling and wonder if this means I'm a success.

I will have no way of knowing what success means, how to judge. Since I am alone in my apartment staring at my ceiling, I cannot be certain.

My little pink book will be number one on *The New York Times* best seller list for months. I will keep my refrigerator empty to remind me not to be so hard on myself, which will not make sense to anyone but me. But it will make sense. One of the oddest things will be that first check. The big payola. When the money comes and I go to deposit it I will have the odd feeling that the woman at the counter is shocked to see my balance over $800. It'll be that high only right before I pay my rent and then it will go back down to the normal one or so hundred. I'll see her staring at the balance line wondering if she's accidentally punched up someone else's account on the computer. But she double-checks and it's me. It's right. I'll take a deep breath.

I won't know what to do with the money so I won't do anything. I'll go home. I won't feel guilty about going to a full-price movie. I'll buy the expensive organic peaches at Whole Foods Market. And inside my apartment, I'll sit in the middle of my living room on the floor—because I prefer it to the couch—and eat my organic peach and stare out the window and watch the lights come on in the homes across the street. The mailman will walk by and I will take a bite of peach.

I will stare out my windows, to the house across the street, a Victorian-looking thing with big bay windows. I won't see anything except the fuzzy glow of TV, but I'll like that it's a home and that a family lives there. While I eat my peach I will wonder if I will ever have a home of my own. I won't get it that I'll be able to afford one. A modest one, say, in the middle of nowhere with two bedrooms and one full bathroom. I will lie back on the floor and close my eyes.

The book I will write will never reveal the truth about me. Instead it will encapsulate everything I wish I were. It will not tell my readers that I do not have any friends, the kind who call you up and ask how you are. It will not reveal how my friends are the sort of friends who say we "used to be so close" and "my best friend from high school,"

those sort of past-tense relationships that people use to make themselves feel better. I won't even mention the ones who call me up only
when they need something. My book will not have witty metaphors
for my loneliness the way some authors do. Instead, my little pink
book will mask all of this; it will make people think that I have always
been this lovable thing, this person everyone wanted to know but didn't.
I will not let my fans know, especially the ones just like me, that, in
fact, I am paralyzed. That I feel this wound inside me that I can't seem
to shake, as if something was torn out of me when I was too young to
remember. And I won't connect this to my grandfather because this is
something I will never think about. I will only know that no matter
how hard I try, I cannot bridge the space between myself and others.
That I am terrified by the prospect of knowing anyone.

I will think about my friends. The ones I called "friend." And I will
wonder about fiends, about the missing "r." What is it about one
small shift that can change an entire structure? I will wonder if it's
worth it. Whether the book I will write will be worth it. Will it be
worth it to be known?

Pink shoes, pink hats, pink umbrella. Pink slipcovers for the couch
and curtains. Pink-colored candles that line a bathtub, pink throw
mats, and pink frames for paintings. Pink mugs, pink forks, pink refrigerator. Pink highlights in a Persian carpet, pink-colored scarves.
All the pink you can eat.

Mr. Spielberg, who of course will fall in love with pink on his first
read, will call me up and leave a message that he wants to "do" pink.
He will say that he is calling from the gym (and I will be able to tell by
the panting) and that he wants me to come out to LA. He'll say, "Call
me back, I want to see you by the end of the week." Mr. Spielberg will
be hard to reach but his assistants will assure me that yes, yes it's in
the hopper. I will wonder about the word *hopper*. 1. a person or thing
that hops. 2. any hopping insect. 3. a box, tank, or other container, often funnel-shaped, from which the contents can be emptied slowly
and evenly.

Mr. Spielberg's assistant will be named Alison or James or Henrietta. It will keep changing because so many people work for him that every time I call I get another assistant, so I will collectively call them Henry, but never directly. Henry will always answer on the third ring, this way I will always know they're busy. Henry will say *hopper* again and something about fabulous. Pink and fabulous and chenille.

When I get to California, Mr. Spielberg will be nicer than I expect. The book I will write will be in his right hand and he will be thumbing through it with his left while a crew of young people hover around him wondering whether or not they should know me. So they don't say anything directly to me until after he does. When they realize I'm the author of the little pink book they will run and get me bottled water in a mug. There will be a rainbow on the mug and it will say, "California! The Place of Dreams."

I will get sick of California quickly, except I will like Venice Beach, because even if it is California it's dirty enough to look like it doesn't belong. I will take long walks in the morning along the boardwalk before any of the vendors have set up, when there are men still asleep, curled on a bench between the ocean and the homes, and everything will seem as it should, as if I were a part of the scene, a figure walking confidently alone in the morning, maybe with a cup of coffee in my hand, and the steam escaping up into the seventy-something-degree weather. But I will be due in Hollywood at an appointed time so I will never feel as if I've gotten to walk quite as long as I would like.

My book will be displayed in the window of the last shop I walk past on the way back so that I will be reminded of purpose. I will realize, briefly perhaps, that the book is just this thing and not who I am at all. But then, I'll be in LA, and Spielberg will be waiting, and they'll be casting actors, and I'll forget all about it within an hour.

After the fifth or sixth trip between Chicago and LA and repeated begging by a Henry, I will decide to get an apartment in Venice Beach. Henry will keep saying, "Wouldn't you be more comfortable in your own place, not just a hotel?" I will think about it and think that I'm just fine with hotels, but that maybe that's the wrong answer, so I will say, "Yes, why yes, of course I'd be more comfortable in my own place." So I will find the place on Bernard, off of Rose Avenue. It'll be cheap and about nine or ten blocks from the beach. I'll have an attic room in a house that a couple owns. I'll have to climb up a ladder to get to my room that is so small it does not even qualify as small, but, rather, tiny. The sloping ceiling will make it so that I can slide a mattress only on one side. I'll bring up a tiny table and matching chair that I'll shove under the one bay window facing the ocean, and it will fit exactly. I'll have piles of books and that'll be it. The couple will let me hang my clothes in a closet downstairs, the one with all the cleaning supplies. I will vow to never let anyone see my room because I won't want to answer why I chose this when I can clearly afford better.

Perhaps after the book I will write is published I will think back to Tucson and my days there in college, about how I wanted to be a poet so bad it hurt my bones. I will not know if it was the age or the place. All that angst and lust. Booze. Maybe it was just the heat because it was always so damned hot. College was a four-year blur. But I will certainly remember one girl. The one who snubbed me, the one who I've technically never met and whose name I never knew, the one who I've always simply referred to as "evil review girl." It was the first and only reading I ever gave. I made up little chapbooks to pass out. Back then it didn't seem vain or anything, just like, why the hell not, right? Turns out the local newspaper sent a student intern to cover the event. The next day I went to pick up a paper to see what they wrote and there it was in black and white: "Junior Poet Doldrums." The article was a full body slam; I dropped out of my poetry class the next day. I was horrified. I jumped in my '68 Rambler and headed out into the desert. I remember crying and crying and that stupid desert expanse. I remember thinking maybe a scorpion could just sting me and I'd be done with the whole thing.

I was dramatic like that.

After the book I will write is published I will not even realize how petty I can be. I will have images of evil review girl reading my little pink book and not even know I am dreaming of my ultimate come-back, which no one will even realize is a comeback except me. I will want to be adored. I will want adoration. But I will never say it out loud. Instead, I will skip reviews altogether and just pretend they're all good.

After I've moved into the attic in Venice I will climb up my ladder into my new room and sit at my desk. I will feel comfortable there, alone in that tiny space. I will stare out at the sky, that tiny shred of a sky.

My mother will call every day wanting to know whom I've spotted. I will say lots of folks only I can't remember their names. She'll be an-noyed by my lack of attention to details. I'll save myself by telling her that at the Rose Cafe I saw Richard Gere and that will impress her.

At the studio **Mr.** Spielberg will talk about the bane of the paparazzi, but I will always smile for the cameras. In fact, I will not try to run from the press whatsoever. I will stand very patiently while they spell out my name and ask questions like, "So what's Spielberg like? Is it true you're sleeping with him?" This of course is absurd, but they know it and ask regardless. They've got to get sex involved. I will say, "Hellllloooo, *pink?*" I will think that the *pink* would say it all, but because they won't get it and my mother won't want to get it, I will invent a lover. My mom will be thrilled, as will my friends who were convinced I'd always be alone.

My imaginary lover will find me because of the book, which he got as a gift from an ex-girlfriend who thought he needed something in-tellectual in his life. The only reason he read it was because his buddy at the gym, the guy who did free weights next to him, said his girl told him to read it. Out of sheer boredom the guy picked it up while he was on the pot one night and sat in the bathroom all night and read the damn book. Can you imagine?

So my imaginary lover will go out and get it and read the whole thing, cover to cover, something he never does. Then later on, say a week later, I'll be walking down along the strip in Venice, like usual, and he'll be jogging by and recognize me from the cover. Only he'll think it's a mistake because he's sure I live in Chicago. So he'll go home and I'll keep walking and nothing will happen at all. Except the next morning, it'll be the same thing. I'll be walking, he'll be running, and he'll stop and ask, "Did you write that book?" I'll look at the ground because I'm nervous. I'll drag my toe across the cement in front of me and answer him. "Yes."

He'll ask, "But what are you doing here, in Venice?" That's when I'll have to tell him about the movie and all the rigmarole, but it won't sound pretentious because there's no one around. The coffee in my hand will burn my skin, and I'll keep moving the cup from one hand to the other while I'm trying to tell him about it. He'll laugh and finally take the cup from me and hold it while I talk. It will seem like the sweetest gesture I've ever seen, even though it's not.

But then, lo and behold, a few weeks later I'll see him again. Only this time he'll be on a date. I'll have to say hi. So I will. Casual. (This is the part my mother will especially like, the crowd-pleaser part, the part where everyone cheers because they will want to believe in this.) I'll walk past his table and the woman will look at me, which will cause him to look at me. Then I'll smile and he'll remember our conversation. I'll say, "It's good to see you" as I'm walking away. I'll be out the door but he'll get up and make some lame excuse to his date and will follow me out. He'll say, "Wait" (and this is because I've always wanted someone to say wait, just wait). My mother will love it, and even though it's a lie, I will somehow think it's not a very bad one, I mean, everyone will be happy. The media, my parents, my friends. However, I will wonder who, exactly, I am. I will feel more like an alien than myself. And I will wonder about the word *self*. But I won't have much time to consider this, only every once in a while.

My little pink book will be hyped by Oprah Winfrey, so I'll have to fly from California back to my hometown, Chicago. She will introduce the book and cross her legs, adjusting the clip-on microphone and say, "With me today is the writer of this magnificent little book." She will hold it up in front of her so that everyone tuning in can write down the name and go out and buy it. I will walk onto the stage slowly, feeling a little odd to be on the *Oprah Winfrey Show*. How strange! I will wear jeans because I will want to seem everyday-like. Ordinary. But when I smile the audience will see me. I will thank her profusely for inviting me. When she gets up to greet me I will wonder if I should extend my hand for her to shake or if I should hug her. What will seem more proper?

Someone in the audience will ask me if I believe that writers have to suffer in order to write. I will stare out at the audience and the hot, hot lights and I will wonder how much I am sweating. I will wonder about suffering, sweat, suffocation, about which angle she means. I will think about my grandfather, about my imaginary lover that I would like to kill off, about pink. I will say, "No, no, of course not!" And in that moment I will believe it, because I will know that my suffering is mostly of my own doing, that I chose to be alone. Another woman will say it's so deep, she couldn't believe it. She's not sure she understood it all. This will make me think of black holes and hurricanes, and I will think about the commercials they'll run when it airs. I will wonder about product development and market penetration. Oprah will be majestic and she will wear pink in honor of my book. We will talk about starving kids in Africa and starving Tibetan monks in India. She will lean in close to me and say, "Did you suffer all those years trying and trying but only getting rejection after rejection?" I will wonder if she is talking about my writing or my love life. There's very little difference. The reporter from New York will love it. When the book I will write is published everyone will want my dirt, but I'll only give them pink.

When the *Oprah* show airs my mother will tape the whole thing and send it to my grandfather, who will invite the whole neighborhood over to watch it. Only, since almost everyone is dead, there will be only a bunch of ninety-year-olds in front of the VCR watching it play over and over. He will call afterward and tell my mother how great it is that Oprah had me on, how good I looked sitting next to her. I won't care. I'll go back to my crappy old apartment in Chicago and order pizza. Cheese and pepperoni. I'll try to think of someone to call and tell everything that's happening, but since they've all read about it in the papers, they'll all know. So there'll be nothing to say. So I'll go to the bathroom and run the water in the tub and climb in.

I will think about my grandfather and those paralyzing dreams. The ones where I am climbing up to an attic and the space gets narrower and narrower and I can't breathe and the door handle glows all silvery like some Stephen King movie in which you know the monster is waiting there for you just beyond the door. I will grab at my neck and remember feeling like I am choking, like I am somehow dirty and choking all at once, and I will sink under the water in the tub. I will try to forget. I will remember how everyone loves my grandfather. Everyone does. He is jolly. He is kind. That's what everyone says. The ladies in the supermarket say "I just *love* your grandfather, he's such a sweet old guy." The ladies at church in their pillbox hats exclaim, "Oooooh, he's so cute I could just pinch him!" I will remember pink and think it's not so bad. I will say it's just the memory of a dream, that's all. I will try to believe this as I let the water absolve me. My little pink book will be number one. I will be someone worthwhile.

My grandfather will call me and I will answer my cell phone on the second ring. He will tell me all about his dentures that are coming loose, but because they are coming loose his words will be jumbled and unclear and I will get what he's saying only because I can't understand what it is he's saying. He will ask me how it is in California. Is it any different? I will tell him the weather is great: a balmy eighty-three degrees (because it will always be summer). I will tell him about Cassiopeia and Pleiades, the way they hang in the sky, how I sometimes can see them from the beach, and how I stay up to watch them shift across horizon. But this will be a lie because in Venice I will hardly be able to see the Little Dipper with all the smog. He will say there are rumors that I've been abducted by aliens. He'll have read it in the grocery store. He will say, "You haven't seen any aliens have you?" I will hang up the phone with this dreadful pit in my stomach that I can't explain. I will feel like vomiting. I will want to cry.

My imaginary lover will end up running off with the guy from his gym. The one who stood next to him while they did free weights, who sat on his toilet all night reading my book. My mother will find out when she is reading the newspaper one morning, between bites of chocolate chip ice cream, thumbing through the Metro section. She'll call me up straight away. I'll have to think fast. It'll be unfortunate that I can't fake crying. She will be instantly suspicious by my lack of concern. I'll wonder if she knows I'm a lesbian. I'll shrug her off, though since we're on the phone she won't know this. I will say he wasn't really the one for me. She will bring up the fact that I am thirty-two, like I'm going to shrivel up and keel over. She'll say, "Couldn't you tell he was gay? Don't they have that radar thing? Weren't there any signs at all? And what about his friends?" I won't get a word in, so I'll let her talk to herself for a while and rest the phone in the crook of my neck. When I hear a pause, I'll say, "You know, he did wear a lot of pink, but I thought it was to flatter me."

The fact that my imaginary lover ran off will be widely publicized—not that he was imaginary, just that he ran off. *People* magazine will do an article on couples and a picture of me walking alone along Venice Beach will be featured with a caption that reads "Even though she's sold over a million copies of that little pink book, this lady still walks alone." Of course, since there never were any pictures of him and me together, because of the impossible nature of it, they won't be able to run a picture of us together. Nor will they be able to run one of those pictures that has a red slash through the middle, or a picture that's ripped in two where the lovers were once glued together.

My imaginary lover would not have been any particular type. Rather, bits of this person and bits of that. He would have had a profile you can recognize in a crowd. My lover wouldn't have been the type of person who would blend. He would have had the same hair as the first girl I had a crush on as a teen. Maybe her eyes too. My imaginary lover would have known things about me I didn't like to admit and would have loved me regardless. Mostly, my imaginary lover would not have minded that I am a little insane. For example, he wouldn't mind that I like guacamole but not avocados and don't like to eat sandwiches but like all the stuff that goes inside them. He'd overlook that I worry so much over the fact that friend is spelled dangerously close to fiend. My imaginary lover would not have even tried to hold my hand because he'd have known that I'm a homo and just needed a cover. He'd have been that beard.

I will get e-mails from gossip columnists asking to confirm the name of the gym my imaginary lover and his lover worked out in and whether or not the other guy was a model. There will be sightings of my imaginary lover all throughout Los Angeles. My imaginary lover on Rollerblades near Zuma Beach. My imaginary lover and his new lover standing along the boardwalk in Santa Monica watching as David Hasselhoff films *Baywatch,* which will instantly prove his moral inferiority to my friends, who will be trying to console me over the loss of my imaginary lover. I will want to stick up for him. I will want to say things like, "If only you knew him. He was kind!"

On my walk back from the beach one day I will realize how lucky I was that *The National Enquirer* was the one who broke the story about my imaginary lover being imaginary. This will be months after the fact, but still, you never know when these things can pop back up. I will know that my mother suspects that the tabloid, for once, is correct. I will have no proof. I will have squat.

I will often meander along the boardwalk in Venice and contemplate my nonexistent love life. Certainly I will have more options. After all, I'll be published. But the point won't be about options, it will be about pink. How much can I stand? Am I willing to let me be pink? I will decide to think of myself as a monk in training. I will be celibate. I won't be able to tell my mother this because she will already have me marrying Brad Pitt in the Bahamas. She won't care that he's a media circus or that I'm a lesbian.

I'll keep trying to tell her that he doesn't do it for me, but she won't get it. She'll say, "He's Brad Pitt. I mean *Brad Pitt,*" and she will say it slowly, and draw it out. But still, I'll say, "Mom you don't get it." I'll want to tell her that I need someone who doesn't mind that I prefer to be invisible. Someone who gets it. A girl. But I won't, instead I will slide the phone away from my mouth and say, "Mother, don't you know I'm . . . whatever." And she will say, "What did you say?" I will say, "Nothing, nothing," and hang up. I will be terribly relieved when my imaginary lover runs off with his gym partner.

At sunset the sky in LA will be the shade of pink that is my second choice for the cover of the book I will write. Rose or blushing fuchsia. All those shades of pink swirling together: mauve, dusky pale rose like fading firecracker smoke, pale bits of lavender. And the sun at sunset will be this burning globe in the lower right-hand corner of the sky.

TWO

I'll get a call from a Henry, who is worrying about the screenplay I'll be writing. I'll want to do the whole thing myself, but he'll insist I call the editor he's hired to help me adapt my book. But I won't. I will not want to relinquish control, but I will pretend to for a while. I will say things like, "I've surrendered." Meanwhile, the editor, a guy called Nancy, will be waiting on my call and I'll be stuck on page one, which of course is ludicrous. This is the page that everyone will keep asking me about. It will be more famous than "As Gregor Samsa awoke one morning from uneasy dreams" and the rest of it.

That first reporter—the chick from *The New Yorker*—will have asked me how on earth I thought to start it off that way. But see, the first sentence was the easiest. In fact, I almost took it out. She'll have liked that answer quite a bit, so much so that her title will be "The Sentence That was Almost Erased." When I see it in the magazine's table of contents I will want to swoon. I will want to vomit and swoon all at once and won't know what to do. But see, in reality, I will have struggled over that damn sentence for six months, not looked at it for another three, and then have gone back finally and figured it out. But I won't tell her that. I will want to seem natural about my success. Like the jeans and the diner.

The first time I see my book in print I will stand at my mailbox staring at the package from the printer, and I will be afraid to open it. The box will look gigantic even if it is only eight inches long by six inches wide. I will stare at the return address, at my name on the label and my own address and it won't seem possible that I'm holding this thing in my hands, that it exists. I won't want to open it. I will want to wait, but I will rip it open the second I get back inside my apartment. I will grab a knife because I can't find my scissors and I will plunge the tip of it deep into the cardboard, but not deep enough to gouge the book accidentally. Then I will slide the blade all the way down the length of the package and open it up. The bright pink will remind

Pink
doi:10.1300/5768_02

me of cotton candy the way I thought it might. I will also think of ribbon and gifts and figure those are good things too.

I will stare at that picture of me on the cover standing in the middle
of the desert, with my arms extended as far apart as I can get them, as
if I could grab hold of the sky and keep it. I will think back to when
they took it—no to before that really, to the plane ride going out to
Tucson. I'd sit in row 18, in a window seat. The whole time we're up
in the air I would stare out the window and watch the wing of the
plane cut through the sky and wonder how much the sky weighs.
Does it have weight? It takes up space, so I figure it must. I will wonder how scientists determine it. Do they scoop up bits of air with tiny
micro instruments like the shovel I used as a kid to make sand castles,
only infinitely smaller, and put the air into tiny micro test tubes? I'll
stare out the window at the clouds. When I was a child I thought
those clouds held dreams.

The man sitting next to me will not be able to keep still. He will
keep trying to cross his legs, which on a plane doesn't work. So he'll
keep bumping into my legs and shuffling his ass in his seat trying to
get that "just right" position. This will take up most of his time.
Other than his brown plaid shirt I will think he's okay. He'll never introduce himself and I will be glad. Maybe it'll be because of my staring out of the window the whole time. Or maybe he won't like the
look of me. Maybe he'll think I am a spy from the CIA en route to
Mexico. I could be.

I could be anything. But I'm just this girl going to the desert to
take a picture. On the plane on the way out to the desert, I will think
back to my days in college, at the U of A in Tucson, and how I spent
hours and hours alone hiking in that dirt. I will think about the spring
when the water evaporates from the streams running through the
land, and all the moss turning silver, dying, and how the flowers fade
from brilliant hues to half-shades to survive, as if by losing a bit of
color they can cheat death. I will think the desert is a freshly pressed
shirt. Somehow this will make perfect sense.

The way I dream about the desert is the way most folks dream about money. It means change, which is why I'll want it on the cover of the book to begin with: transformation, blossoming. The pink tips of a wildflower. It will never occur to me that I'll pick the desert as a setting merely to spite evil review girl, who, after all, I would barely remember. It was so long ago! It was juvenile! But this is a lie and it will never occur to me to be so spiteful. At least not much.

Although it's true that the book I will write will have nothing to do with self-help, self-love, or self-discovery, the photo will invoke all those things and urge readers to consider their own their own true pink. The photo, like the publication itself, will be accidental. I will say the cover of the book should be "pink" and the publisher's marketing team will say "minimal." The desert will be our go-between.

The man next to me on the plane will not stop fidgeting. I'll watch the land go from bumpy masses of greens and gray as we pass over the Rockies to flat streaks of brown earth as I stare at the stewardess out of the corner of my eye. I'll watch her execute a half turn toward Customer A and say, "What would you like sir?" She'll do a half turn back to the cart, lean down over the drinks, just enough to give Customer A a quick glimpse of cleavage, not quite on purpose, but I won't be sure. She'll make her way up and down the aisle. Half turn, half turn, skin, soda, ice. When she comes to my row I'll ask for a Diet Coke and if I can have the whole can. I'll drink my soda and think about the photo. How should I stand? Should I wear something fancy or plain? Should I smile? If I smile I might look too go-lucky, spacey. If I don't, I might look stern. Unapproachable. I don't want to seem stern but then I don't want to look like a cheerleader either, so I'll decide on a small grin, with the corners of my lips turned slightly up, as if I am somehow detached but pleasantly pleased with the whole experience. The grin will say that the desert is everything I think it will be. It will not say anything about the book.

When the plane touches down in Tucson, I'll be relieved. The photographer's crew will greet me at the gate and laugh as I stumble out behind the man in brown plaid. They'll say for a writer I sure seem normal. By this I'll take it they mean unsuspecting. I'll say, "Why yes,

I am." Neither of them will offer to carry my duffel that keeps tipping me over, so I'll stumble all the way through the airport, repeatedly switching hands, knocking into the oncoming traffic of people.

They'll load me into a Suburban and we'll drive south through miles and miles of empty land. The type of landscape you always drive through, but never stop in. Only we do eventually stop. The only thing there is a lot of is brown and blue. Brown stretches out in all directions. I'll know we are going to Cochise, which is just past Benson but before Tombstone.

When I finally get out of the car I'll walk around in that hot oven air, kick up dirt with the tip of my gym shoe, and watch a lizard skitter toward a bit of brush a few yards away. I will think back to when I was younger, to how I spent so much of my time alone in that desert, watching the clouds pass over. And I will wonder why it is I am always contemplating clouds.

I will open the door and walk out into the desert, and even though it's miserably hot out it will feel good against my arms. The heat will sink into me and I will feel my heart rate slow to match the pace of the heat. The sky will be a huge blue mass. I will feel tiny, and I will remember exactly what I liked so much about the desert. Being tiny. Invisible. I will remember how before the book I will write is published that I loved to be invisible. I was convinced I was and that only if I willed it could you see me. I was invisible most of the time. I sat in my cockroach-infested apartment, in Chicago, willing myself into emptiness. And when I walked along the streets, like Michigan Avenue or Lincoln, I would go past people who would walk right through me. Not around or by, but through. It was convenient really, to be so invisible; I could see everything without guilt or shame. I would walk through stranger's intestines and kidneys. This is how it was before. Before all that pink.

I will want to tell the reporter, the one from *The New Yorker,* that maybe it started in the desert, when I was a junior in college. I will want to tell her the story about evil review girl. I will want to tell her how everyone thought I was so awful back then, so fake. But I won't tell her because it will be too close to the truth. Everyone thought I was a liar and I was. I was. So I will want to talk about myself in the past tense as if I was dying slowly, gracelessly. I will want to say I had friends, once. After the book I will write is published I will want to be dramatic. I will want to say I have a lot of friends. So-and-so and so-and-so. But it will be a lie. I will think back to Cochise Stronghold, this place in the desert that looks like a rock garden, something carved by man. Only man had nothing to do with it. It's this place that is carved by wind and rain, all the elements conspiring together to create this landmark, this pink-shaded rock garden. I will want to tell the reporter about loss. About land and suicide and my two dead brothers. But I will just be quiet. I will keep all this hidden. And when I am talking with the reporter in one of her follow-up calls she will say she thinks there is a lot I'm not telling her. I will use my every-person charm and laugh. I will laugh her off my track. I will talk about the book and pink high heels.

In the desert the photographer will be walking around me in circles saying, "This place is perfect, it's absolutely nowhere." He'll say, "I love it." I will look around and notice that the brown is more of a series of shades of brown like in fancy catalogs in which all the names are less like the names of colors and more like a series of objects: oatmeal, sage, burnt umber, and chocolate. The crew will be busy unloading and setting up equipment. And the photographer will insist on extra lighting, even though the desert is on fire. It'll be so bright it will hurt my eyes, so I'll walk around squinting, holding my hand up over my eyes to shade them from the glare.

After a while the photographer will be shouting at me, but I will be lost in thought. I will marvel that my little pink book has taken me to the middle of nowhere and made me visible in the process. I will wonder about willpower and surrender.

I will start laughing in the middle of the shoot like when I was in second grade and Jimmy Carpenter would poke me in the back and tease me until I burst out laughing. I will laugh hard, and for no reason at all other than sheer nerves. But that is a lie. I will laugh because I cannot cry. I will want to find the nearest closet, any closet will do.

I will want to run back in and shut the door. I will think that maybe I am not ready to be out, to be visible and real.

I will giggle each time he tries to take the picture because I will feel stupid standing in the middle of the desert with my arms wide open. This, of course, will infuriate the photographer, who will yell, "You'd better hurry up; the light will only stay this way for so long." I will feel bad about being difficult, so I will look up at the sky, at the odd color that late in the afternoon turns the color of blue you see in the tail of a peacock, that crazy vibrant blue. The bits of clouds will make me feel less exposed. I will lower my head, turn, and face the camera and pretend I am staring at an imaginary lover who would stand there perfectly still, waiting for me. She would be.

The photographer will pick an assortment of odd poses for me: sitting Indian style, standing with my hands on my hips (I'll like the sassy nature of that one), standing solemnly with my arms straight at my sides, standing with my arms thrown up over my head, and standing with my back to the camera. By the end I will feel entirely overexposed. I will think it must be that the film will simply disintegrate because it's not possible to be so exposed, so raw and known. I will think this isn't what I bargained for. Perhaps, while I'm there for that shoot, I will let myself remember.

In the commotion of picture taking I will look around at the desert surrounding me. There will be something about the long sky that strikes me, the same way an ugly dog pulls at your heart, or how when you meet a certain person it's like you've always known them. I will think maybe I am looking in a mirror, that the desert is me, that I am that lone pale sky. I will see all the living around me: the tiny weeds sprouting up, wildflowers, and all the strange, scrubby cacti that make the land appear hostile. It will all be happening without me, and in that moment I will feel a little better, because it will remind me of writing.

When the photographer gets back the proofs for the cover of the book I will write I will have to fly to New York to meet with him and the publisher. In New York, the photographer will spread all the images out over a mahogany table. My face will lie against the mahogany in black and white. The photographer will hold a magnifying glass up over the pictures so everyone can see my pores and the pimples that could be forming like giant volcanoes. But the men will politely ignore all that, after all, they can airbrush the photo and reinvent me. The sixty shots will swirl over the mahogany and make me dizzy to see so much of myself. The photographer will take his time showing off his work, and after a while I won't look like myself. I will be an image on the paper, my hair floating behind my head, the clouds behind me, and the way I hold my arms out. Extended. I will be a one-dimensional phenomenon.

It will take three hours and twenty-eight minutes for them to realize that it's the first shot the photographer took in the desert that they will use for the cover. In that time, I will have drunk two cups of coffee that someone brought while I wasn't looking and bitten my fingernails all the way down. It will be an obvious choice because in all the others I'll look like a person who is trying very hard not to look like I'm having my photograph taken. I'll look down at the floor and wait for someone to say something. It will be quiet for a good five minutes as the magnifying glass is passed hand to hand. Finally I'll say, "It's the picture with my arms out wide, that's it. It's got to be that one." There will be a small scurry of hands reaching over the table trying to find that image and then a small oooooooh, ahhhhhhh as everyone sighs their agreement. The photographer says, "I knew it. I knew when I took it. Don't you just love the angle?" He preens and picks up the image in his hand and holds it up away from his face, so that everyone can see it. He says yes, yes, yes.

Pink elephants, pink poodles, pink tapioca pudding. Pink in the sky at sunset, pink feathers of a toucan. Pink salamanders, pink fish, pink-colored crayons. Pink pearls, pink buttons on a pink sweater, pink painted toenails.

THREE

When I go on *Oprah* I will decide to shake her hand, figuring I've never been much of a hugger to begin with and I don't want to appear fake on TV. The day she interviews me, my little pink book will have been on the market for exactly a month, long enough for people to see it and for her to have read it. Because it'll have been only a month, I will still be shocked by all the commotion. Backstage, before I go on, I'll sit down and the makeup lady will come over to fix me. She'll have a zillion different colors of base makeup, goopy stuff that she'll smear all over me. I'll wonder if it would have been easier to get a stunt double for the interview. The lady will be indifferent to my small talk. I'll be nervous. I'll be chattering like a fool. My little pink book will sit on the counter next to all the makeup and I'll stare from the makeup to it and back again. I'll have no idea what Oprah is going to say to me, what is expected of me. All I will be able to think of is how my parents told me to say hello to my grandfather, if I could, while I'm on the air.

But I won't want to. I will carry this long-held urge to scream, Why didn't you protect me from him? But this will be only a fleeting thought and the attic, his hands, and the bits of sky that I remember seeping through windows will float away in an instant. I will never let myself think too long.

The first time my mother comes to visit me in California I'll put her up in the Beverly Hills Hotel and won't eat for the next three months. Okay, I will eat, but I will feel like I can't afford to. Since this will be before my imaginary lover runs off with his gym partner, my mother will say she wants to meet him. I won't have too many believable excuses as to why she can't. He's at the gym. He's at work. I never will decide what it is he does. He's doing volunteer work at the hospital. And later on, after the "dumping," my mother will point out that he was a candy striper. She'll say, "Didn't you know he was gay then?" She'll be saying this as we drive around Beverly Hills. I will rent a limo for the few days she's out and we will go everywhere in a big white stretch. She will be asking to see my place, and when we go down to the beach in time for the sunset, I will point in the direction of Topanga Canyon, wave, and say, "Oh, I live over there." I will lie and she will say, "Lovely, just lovely." She will never know about my attic room in the house on Bernard.

My father will be working, but he will call all the time to tell me how great it is that I'm such a success. He'll tell me on my cell phone that my mom is so impressed, that she's told everyone at church how when Oprah called I said I'd have to check my schedule and call back. I'll talk to my dad on the cell phone while Mom and I drive around in the stretch with my mom yelling out the names of streets: Wilshire, 2nd, Ocean Avenue.

My mom will say that we should pull over and get a picture of ourselves on the pier in Santa Monica, so the driver will pull over and stop. We'll walk the length of the pier and my mom will put her arm over my right shoulder, her hand resting on my back, and the two of us will walk out to the end. She'll say, "So tell me, was Richard Gere gorgeous or what? He's gay, isn't he?" And I'll say, "No, he's a Buddhist." She'll want to go to the Rose Cafe. I'll tell her it's just this café, nothing special. She'll say, "But still, if you saw Richard Gere there, I want to go." I will say that he's probably in New York, that he lives there I think. At the end of the pier my mother will lean over the rail and look down at the ocean churning beneath us.

The ocean will be green. The ocean will swell and pitch and heave its way around cement pylons onto the shore. My mother and I will watch whitecaps shift over the top of the water. The wind will lift and pull and shift so that the moisture of the water falls back on us as we stand at the end of the pier.

With all the water falling between us it will be hard to hold on to my anger. I will think about my grandfather and remember the trunks of elephants. That fuzzy wrinkled skin. I will remember when he undid his pants and how I thought his penis looked like the trunk of an elephant, the stuffed one I slept with. I was four or five; I can't remember. I will remember thinking that something was wrong. I will stare down into the churning waves and realize I can't feel anything at all. I will be numb. All these years later. And I will know this is how I've always been.

I will not take my mother on my daily walk along the boardwalk in Venice. Partly because she will be across town in Beverly Hills and partly because she would wonder why I don't go when all the stores are open. So I'll go for my walk and then meet her in the lobby. My mom will stand by the front desk and wait for me to arrive. I'll ask her if she's spotted anyone famous. She'll say the pickings are slim, and we'll go outside and get into the rented stretch limo. We'll drive around some more and go up to Rodeo Drive. We won't be able to afford anything, but we'll stare at it all regardless. I'll say it's a little like wrapping paper at Christmas, isn't it, all those stores lined up? It won't be much of a question though so she won't answer. While she's out she'll say she wants to get her hair done at one of the fancy salons. I'll tell her it's my treat. I'll want to give her everything I can. The driver will suggest a place two blocks up. I'll call and make two appointments so we can go together. My mother will say that maybe the hairdresser will have read my book. I'll say maybe and press down on the button that unrolls the window. The wind will feel good against my face.

At the salon, my mother and I will wear matching plastic drapes that are supposed to keep the dead hair off of us, but it will end up down the back of my shirt regardless. We'll sit next to each other in a line of barber chairs that will look the same as those at the Supercuts store I go to. Two nearly identical looking women will approach us and introduce themselves as Simone and Evan. Evan will cut my mother's hair and Simone will cut mine. I'll ask, "Nina Simone is my favorite singer, are you named after her?" But she won't know who I'm talking about, so I'll sit and stare at myself in the mirror while she cuts my hair. My mother, unable to resist, will tell them both all about my book and how I was recently on *Oprah* and all about Spielberg. I'll be a little embarrassed, but Simone will be instantly impressed and want to talk about the soon-to-be movie. Unlike Evan, Simone is not an actress cutting hair for a living. Simone is a hair specialist, but she will hope to someday do hair for the stars. She'll say

that every once in a while she gets someone famous, like Sylvester
Stallone. She cut his hair the other week. Here my mom will turn to
Simone and ask if he is as short as everyone says. Simone will be so
busy talking about stars and star sightings that my bangs will get
dangerously close to disappearing. I'll look around the salon. There
will be ten other women besides my mother and me who all will be
wearing our identical plastic drapes, facing the mirror, staring at
themselves. My mother will be gabbing with Simone and Evan about
the soon-to-be movie of the book. Then, about ten or so minutes later,
Evan will turn to me and say, "Oh! The little pink book, that's your
book."

Pink triangles. Pink feather boa. Pink stiletto heels, and pink
fishnet stockings. Pink clouds, pink fogs, pink off-the-scale earthquakes. Pink, pink, pink.

After my imaginary lover runs off I will still have to deal with my
mother. I will be afraid of loss. I will remember when I was five and
was first told about my brothers. They're dead, of course. I will remember sitting at the dining room table in our home. A long oblong
thing of dark wood. What I'll remember are the big windows at the
end of the table looking out into the yard. Not unlike my window in
the attic. I will remember holding onto my stuffed elephant and the
way my parents looked at me when I asked why I can't have a brother
or a sister. I will remember the way they held each other as they
spoke, the way they said, "You have two brothers. They're just not
here, that's all." I will remember the way I learned the words *stillbirth*
and *blood transfusion*. Something about our blood fighting with my
mother's blood. I'll remember how my mother said, "You almost died
too, but God loved you so much, he spared you." "So you see," she
said, "you are our gift."

I will remember wondering why I was the one to live. About sur-
vival and what it means to lose all my blood at birth. The only thing
that was mine. I will remember it as the beginning of emptiness.

· Everywhere we go my mother will point out wedding rings on fingers, white cakes, churches, and limos. She will say of the rented limo,

"Something like this would be great for your honeymoon." So I will start to wear pink. Everything pink. Pink bras. Pink undies. Pink dental floss that I will run through my bleeding pink gums. I will wear as much pink as I can fathom putting on. I will rely on subterfuge. My wardrobe will become as bright as Dorothy's golden road in Oz and it will shimmer with pink chemises, pink corduroys, pink leather shoes, pink Converse, and pink mock turtleneck sweaters.

In the lobby of the Beverly Hills Hotel, my mother will sit me down and say, "Wait, just wait" (though this is not the wait, just wait I have been waiting to hear). She will leave and go back to her room. I will wonder what on earth she is doing. I will sit there in the lobby and watch the bellboys pick up strangers' luggage and give those same strangers dirty looks after they've turned their head and walked away. I will watch the people at the front desk smile and say, "How may I help you?" My mother will return carrying the little pink book under her left arm, holding a hatbox in her right. She will sit down in a comfortable chair next to me, put the book on the table between us, and open the hatbox in her lap, which is filled with clippings of brides. All of them in white. I will say, "No, no. I want to get married in pink."

My mother will roll her eyes. She will start pulling out pictures of dresses that she thinks could be appropriate and I won't have the heart to tell her that it's all just a lie so I will watch her point out the difference between a bell hemline and an A-line dress. She will hem and haw over mandarin, round, and scoop-necked dresses. "Honey," she will say, "do you think he'll wear a tux or just a suit?"

She will never be able to see where I begin and she ends, and I will never be able to draw that line between us. What will result is years of embattlement. The two of us, out of nothing but pure love, will construct and destruct ourselves over and over. Yelling and crying and forgiving. I will always go along, and each time I go along my sense of self will slip away that much more, which is why in college I was called a "chameleon" and understand it to be true. I will be furious that I am so passive.

I will remember the time I refused to join the Junior League. My mother said, "But this is what young ladies do. This is how you meet the proper people, make connections." My mother thought I was mentally ill. She thought I hated her because I didn't do what she told me and I didn't know how to tell her otherwise. It did not end well. And because I came to know that what I want results in arguments, I learned how to lie. I will not be proud that I am such a coward, but I will lie and lie and lie.

My mother will have the whole wedding planned three weeks into the lie about my imaginary lover. She will not read the little pink book; she won't even open the cover, so she won't know. Instead she will place it on a shelf in her house, in the living room so that it will be on display but untouched. None of her friends will know the content of the book and no one will ask. They won't want to be rude. They will look at the pink and my name on the side and wonder, but it will all be hush-hush. However, my mother will tell all her friends about Spielberg and the film that will be a must-see and that my imaginary lover lives in Venice, where her daughter (me) got a second apartment, which, she adds, is probably really amazing since it's so close to the beach! She won't know that it's a three-by-five attic with one big bay window that looks into the neighbor's backyard and onto their Astroturf. She won't know how I have to climb up and down a ladder to pee in the middle of the night. She won't know about that. And in the lobby of the Beverley Hills Hotel my mother will hold onto the pictures of her white, white brides and tell me how she's been saving them for me for years.

I will be meeting with one of the Henrys when the book I will write rolls out to 15,000 Borders and Barnes and Noble stores across the country. My very own pink will be out on the shelves in plain sight. I will squirm as I sit with the Henry. I will pull at the neck of my T-shirt and wring my hands. My cuticles will be bloody from biting, so I will try to hide them from Henry, and I will crack my neck so many times that Henry will say, "Do you need to see a specialist for that?" I will wonder if I am having an anxiety attack. I will wonder what an anxiety attack looks like and whether or not this is one. Henry will explain Mr.

Spielberg's process for making the book I will write into a movie. We are having coffee at my favorite café, not far from my attic on Bernard. The Novel Cafe, on Pier Avenue, just off Main. I will have found it by accident.

The Henry says, "I need one hundred and twenty-five pages in three weeks. Can you deliver?" Henry sits there looking at me as if I am a delivery boy driving around crates of milk. It is clear he expects that I can, so I nod my head. "Why yes, of course I can, of course!" What's 125 pages? What's a little layout change and revamping? It can't be that much.

Henry will look around the Novel Cafe and say, "Why do you like this joint? It's a dump." I'll say "No, no, it's quaint." And it is. There are old dusty books everywhere, and it's one of the few remaining vintage-style cafés in LA, if not the entire United States. After the book I will write comes out and I have money of my own I will still dress more like a slacker than a success. I will prefer my disheveled hair to any salon do, and I will ignore the fact that I'm too old for that disheveled poet look. I will scoff at anyone who says so, but will not do so out loud. I will consider being "put-together" as bourgeois, so I will insist on being unkempt. But I will recognize a thread of neurosis about this, so I will be willing to negotiate, like when I have to go on photo shoots or do the TV shows like Oprah's and Barbara Walters. No one will suspect that this is related to homegrown cafés versus chains like Starbucks or Caribou, but there will be a direct correlation, which would be clear if people knew.

Henry will sit in the Novel Cafe and look out of place. He will be telling me things about writing a screenplay, talking about software I can get to help with the layout and style, and he'll be sure that I am listening, but I won't be—not because I'm uninterested, but because things would have just spun madly out of control in my mind. I would be obsessing on the books being delivered across the country. Which way would they be placed on the shelves? Would there be displays? Would the book I will write be prominently displayed or just moderately so? Henry will say things like, "There's a lot of heat on this; we've got to get moving." He will remind me about the editor, Nancy, who's waiting to hear from me. Henry gestures toward himself and says, "I'm synonymous with Mr. Spielberg. I'm like your personal pager. Call if you get stuck or whatever." Henry will be a papier-mâché figure on exhibit and I will be floating away.

Some things will not change once the book I will write is published. For instance, I will cry just as much over my mother's clipped-out magazine brides when I am back upstairs, alone in my attic, and it will hurt just as much when a week later my mother calls to tell me my grandfather is dying. And at his funeral I will cry the same amount, regardless of the book I will write, and I will wear the same black dress.

FOUR

It will be sunny and warm and I will be angry that there are so few clouds in the sky. There should always be clouds when someone is dying. And the walls of the houses on Bernard will look terribly dense, as if they were suddenly much heavier. The stucco will not be stucco but weight, and everything will feel like it weighs too much. The air itself will be made of blunt metal. It will be ironic that the sun is so bright and glaring, and perhaps at that moment I will realize that the loss of one life is not so much reflected in nature but absorbed. But maybe this is too philosophical for someone grieving to think of, so perhaps I will have only the notion of this without the means to understand it.

My mother will call from Chicago and make me promise that I will come for the funeral. She'll want me to come home right then: immediate. We'll hang up the phone and I'll finish my glass of tea. One of the Henrys will be sitting at my desk staring out my bay window at the neighbor's Astroturf, and I will be sitting on my tiny bed. We will be talking about how to film the little pink book. He will say things like, "Mr. Spielberg wants to keep it authentic." He will talk about a montage series or perhaps a series of short films put together to make one long film. He'll say things like "impromptu" and "cutting edge." Henry will see this as his chance to get on Spielberg's good side. Henry will be hoping to become like one of Spielberg's adopted kids. He'll be an expert at making himself useful. All of the Henrys will be the same in that regard. Henry will talk about handheld cameras and Super 8 film. I will say, "Great, great, it all sounds great." I will tell him, "I have to pack a bag. I need to leave now. I'm sorry, can you drive me to the airport?" And Henry, even though he is an assistant, will cock his head to one side and have a confused look, as if it is beneath him to take me to the airport. But then he will say, "Yes, yes of course, my car is outside." And Henry, being desperate to devise the perfect film sequence, will ask if he can stay in my attic while I'm gone. He says he wants to absorb it all. He'll lie and say the place is inspiring! But I will know he just wants brownie points. I will know the Henrys and I are a lot alike.

Pink
© 2007 by The Haworth Press, Inc. All rights reserved.
doi:10.1300/5768_04

I will be waiting in line at the airport to buy a ticket to go home for my grandfather's funeral. I will be exhausted at this point. So when a twenty-year-old girl comes up and asks me to autograph her little pink book, it will be no wonder that I burst out crying. I will create quite a scene in the airport. The poor girl will look around and say in a small voice, "All I wanted was an autograph." But everyone will give her dirty looks as if she made me cry. So I will grab her hand and say, "I'm sorry, I'm so sorry, my grandfather is dying." And then I'll reach for the book that's in her other hand, take it from her, and sign it saying, "With love."

I will have an hour to kill in the airport. So I will go to the McDonald's and get a sundae. I will ask if they have chocolate sprinkles because nothing can be too bad with sprinkles. But they don't, so I'll take my plain sundae and walk up and down the terminal aisles. I stare at the families seated in stiff rows of chairs, who are staring at TV screens overhead or out the big windows at the planes on the ground. I walk slow letting all the sounds swirl around me. I will feel as if I'm inside a washing machine: all the dirty clothes and suds going around and around me, tangling around my neck, drowning me. I will stare at the cardboard families sitting perfectly straight and the lone businessmen waiting and waiting. I do not fit into either category. It makes me want to do math equations. $A + B = C$ but $C + A$ does not equal B. Over the loudspeaker a tin voice asks if I've left any bags unattended.

It will be a very different plane ride than the one I took to the desert for the cover of my book. On the plane ride to see my grandfather for presumably the last time, I will not look with wonder at the clouds, nor will I stare out at the blue and contemplate its vastness. Through the airplane window I will look down at the patchwork land, at all the families divided into small plots. I will wonder about boundaries and lines and fitting in the square divisions.

I will try to think of the first memory I have of my grandfather, but, being unable to, I will think he is like the sea. I won't dwell too long on this. I will order my can of Diet Coke as usual and try to distract myself from his impending death. I will have a jumble of feelings that I cannot discern. I will think about the pink of my book and try to fake a smile so that I can see myself smiling in the reflection of the plastic window next to me.

On this trip a young woman sits next to me. She will be skinny and sit quiet still but talk eighty miles a minute. I'll figure she must be from a small town because she talks so fast and about nothing at all. I will figure she hasn't traveled much. She will be a lot like me before the book I will write is published and that will annoy me. While she chatters I will think of things to say to shut her up, none of which I would ever actually say out loud, but I will be grieving and therefore be less aware of how mean my thoughts can be.

The girl will be obsessed with a boy who does not love her. His name will be Barry and she will talk about him for three-fourths of the flight. Barry will be in her physics class. The skinny girl, I'll decide, is in junior college. Barry sat two rows back and one seat to her right, when she was facing forward. I will tune out somewhere after "Barry was seeing Suzanne" and come back in at "I was so drunk you'd never believe it." Though, since I won't know what she's talking about I will be able to believe it. The skinny girl won't miss a beat in her story when the stewardess asks what she would like to eat: pizza or chicken? The skinny girl will say, "Barry was so sweet—chicken—he practically carried me the whole way home." She will stay on her drunk tangent for a long time. Finally, in the middle of her and Barry having sex, I will lean over and say, "My grandfather is dying." That's it. I won't elaborate. I'll say it and turn and stare out the window for the last third of the flight.

If my grandfather hadn't lived to be ninety-eight there would have been a lot more people at his funeral. But since he outlived his wife and nearly all his friends it will be just my mother, my father, the minister, and me. In the plane, over the middle of the Midwest, I will suddenly miss my grandfather's phone calls, like when he called to tell me that Old Harry, whom I didn't know, died at ninety-two while he was in the shower.

My grandfather will die while I'm on the plane listening to the skinny girl next to me. Not knowing whom to call, my mother will call the fire department, an ambulance, and a guy from the morgue, who will all show up at the exact same time. She will not call me. Their street will be humming with sirens and I will be 15,000 feet above it all, staring down, trying to pick out where it is they live among the similar square blocks of land. And because my grandfather will die while I am on the plane, no one will be at the airport to pick me up.

I will try to call home, but no one will answer, and I'll wait for another hour or so at O'Hare, but no one will come. Eventually I will go and take the Blue El Line to Damen in Bucktown on the west side of Chicago, and then I will transfer and take the North Avenue bus east to Wells Street in Old Town. I will grumble the four or so blocks north to my old apartment at the corner of Lincoln and Wisconsin. I will unlock the door and go in and I will not suspect that my grandfather is already dead, because even when you see these things coming, somehow you never expect them when they happen. Like when James's roommate, Franke, the one who will work for the publishing company in New York, calls and tells me she is going to give the manuscript to her boss. I will have already sent the book I will write to six or seven publishers and will be waiting for the rejections. It will turn out to be this strange fluke of James showing the work to his roommate that caused it all to happen. And even though I'll know my grandfather is dying, I will not suspect that he is already dead.

At the funeral I will wonder how it is all connected. The day of my grandfather's funeral, my little pink book will not feel like such a big deal. When the *Today* show calls because they're doing a series on death and dying I will refuse to be one of their guest stars. I will say, "I'm sorry but my grandfather's funeral is today, in about an hour, I can't think past that." The secretary will be nice and apologize for calling at such an awful time. I will say, "It's not awful, it's just a time, but he's dead, see?"

My one black dress will be hanging next to my grandmother's old fur coat I inherited, which my grandfather bought in 1938. It is short, comes to my hips, and has a wide collar that tapers all the way down to the bottom. I guess it's made out of fox or something, maybe beaver. Who can tell? I don't know anything about fur coats and think they're creepy, so I'll push it away from my dress and look at the other things in my closet. It could be a tiny museum.

There on the shelf above my dresses are old copies of the manuscript, coffee-stained things that should be tossed. Old shoe boxes from college and a hat box, also inherited, is crammed way back, just out of reach. I'll pull out the hatbox and sit down on my living room floor and open the lid. The box is filled with photographs of my mother's family. There she is when she was twelve, twirling a baton. There's my grandmother nursing my mother. The black and white of the photo is slightly yellowed, but there in my hand is my mother before she did anything other than open her eyes. My grandfather was obviously the family photographer, because there's only one picture of him. I pull it out. On the back of the photo it says, "Christmas Dinner 1946." My grandfather is standing by the window, behind the dinning room table, although he's not—as I might have suspected from the title of the shot—carving the turkey or standing at the head of the table. Instead, my grandfather is standing next to the window, standing and staring outside with his hands loose at his sides. It's obvious he has no idea anyone has taken the picture. For a moment, I will pause and feel a connection to this man. I will, for the first time in years, allow myself to feel something. I will hold onto that picture and cry. I will slip down to my knees and cry and cry and cry. But I will be crying only in part for him. I will know that I am crying for him and that five-year-old girl that was me. I will hold onto that picture and see him how he was: imperfect, human.

At the funeral, I will stand next to my mother, between my mother and father. There won't be any news reporters trying to get pictures of me grieving, nor will there be television crews live at the scene. It will just be my parents, the minister, and me. In Los Angeles, a Henry will be pacing around his living room with his cell phone in his hand, freaking out about the screenplay and his job, trying to figure out whether or not he should call me and see where I'm at. All of the

Henrys will be sick with fear. They will be calling one another, snapping out orders, trying to assert their power. One Henry will say to another, "No, Spielberg said I'm in control!" The Henrys will have a power struggle the likes of which hasn't been seen since Watergate. And, meanwhile, that lone Henry will still be sitting in my tiny attic, lying back on my mattress, counting cracks in the ceiling, staring out toward the great Pacific. Henry will be imagining what the little pink book will look like on film. He will be thinking about his name in the credits and his next role in the next project. He will be dreaming about power and power and power. Henry will call Mr. Spielberg and say, "I think maybe it's about loneliness, rejection." Henry will say, "We've got to find images of space. Big empty things. Like maybe the desert." And all the other Henrys will be having a meltdown because I haven't yet finished the script.

For whatever stupid reason, I will have brought my cell phone to the graveyard. It will be my grown-up version of a security blanket. The minister will be in the middle of "take this body O Lord" or something like that and my parents will be crying and my cell phone will ring inside the purse I will be carrying. I will wonder if I should answer or not. Who could it be? It might be extremely important, like maybe my book has won an award. And even though I've said the book I will write does not seem terribly important at my grandfather's funeral, it will be important enough. Unable to resist, I will pull it out of my bag and the minister will pause in mid sentence while I say, "Hello?"

I will turn my back to the minister, and my mother will be so shocked she won't do anything at all, and my father's face will turn the fuchsia color that tells me he's so mad I might as well be the one in the grave. I will say, "Who is this?" A Henry will cough and say, "Oh, it's me. When are you coming back? We've got a lot of work you know, the deadline is almost here." I'll say, "Oh God, I can't believe you." Though it's me I will not believe. I'll whisper, "Listen, I'm standing next to the grave and the minister is talking. Can I call you later?"

I will know that answering the phone was rude. Outrageously rude, but I will know that I did it because, despite not wanting to be angry, I am in fact angry at my grandfather. I will want to tell the minister that his words are a waste of time. I will want to be a victim. But I will know I am being petty and that he's just dead and there's nothing I can do to take any of it back. So I will slip the cell phone back into my purse and go back to pretending to listen. The only reason my answering the phone will not actually result in a huge fight is because my grandfather is dead. So I will give him one last thanks in my mind. At my grandfather's house my mother will say we should sort through his stuff now instead of letting it sit. I'll go into the kitchen and get the garbage bags that are kept underneath the sink. We'll start in his room, with the bureau. By the time we are done, there will be eight Hefty bags for the Salvation Army and three for the garbage. The ones for the garbage will have stuff like dried-out nail polish of my grandmother's from who knows what decade, worn boxer underwear that my grandfather will have never got around to throwing out himself, and my grandmother's diaphragm that we'll find in the third drawer from the bottom. I will not mention the little pink book or the screenplay that will be due to Spielberg in exactly five days. I will not mention my block or the fact that I am so far behind. After the book I will write is published I will have no idea how to write the script and will be too proud to ask for help.

Lying in bed that night, back in my old apartment, I will stare out my window and think back to childhood. I will remember all the hours I spent staring at lightning bugs. I will remember how I was so convinced of the Loch Ness Monster. I will think of random things like that. I will sit up in bed and reach over to the bedside table and grab my cell phone.

Henry will answer on the first ring. I will tell him that I'm flying back tomorrow afternoon. I'll say, "Let's meet at the Novel Cafe, okay?" He will groan but agree. I will say, "I'm not sure how it should go, the script, I'm not sure how to make it a film. What does it look like?" And Henry will laugh and say, "I know, I know, why do you think I'm here in your crappy attic?" The book I will write will soar off the pages. It will be a rollercoaster of words, a mantra. It will be no more than a series of words. It will be an anthem.

FIVE

The day after my grandfather's funeral, my parents will drive me to the airport and I'll fly back to LA and my tiny attic. I'll unpack. I'll sit down at the desk. Not much will be different. Henry will have left me a note on my laptop: *Welcome back to the land of palms! This pink thing will work out. I've had a vision!*

I'll take my laptop and paper to doodle on and head out to the Novel Cafe. I'll walk west on Rose to Main Street and north to the café on Pier. Henry will not be there yet, so I'll pick out a table and set up my computer. I'll purposely sit across from this one particular woman who is good to look at in a superficial way.

The lady will be scratching her head and staring at the screen of her laptop. She'll have big goofy glasses, the type Buddy Holly wore in the 1950s. I love Buddy Holly or I would if he were alive and a woman, but since he's dead I just love his music. So I'll instantly like the girl who reminds me of Buddy Holly, though it will be due only to the glasses. I'll decide right then to call her Buddy Holly. Buddy won't look up at me for at least ten minutes, and this will drive me nuts because I'll be sitting there, trying to look studious, and all she'll do is stare at her computer. But when she looks up, she'll look at me like she's not looking at me. You know, she'll look like she's is looking over my left shoulder, at the person walking past me. However, she will be looking at me. The person walking past me will be Henry, who will come around the side of the table and say, loud enough for Buddy to hear, "I don't see why on earth it had to be this joint again."

Buddy Holly will stare at me with the most curious look. She will stare and stare. I won't get it that she actually knows me because she will not look familiar. I will have no memory of our one meeting because I would have been in a blackout, too drunk to remember anything at all. Buddy Holly on the other hand will know exactly who I am. She will remember the kiss. She will remember back to college and some random kiss behind a café with some girl she didn't know, some girl who was so wasted Buddy was afraid the girl would puke in

Pink
© 2007 by The Haworth Press, Inc. All rights reserved.
doi:10.1300/5768_05

her mouth. Buddy will remember watching the *Oprah* show and re-member the little pink book when it first came out. She will remem-ber how in that moment, while I was there shaking Oprah's hand in her studio, Buddy would put it all together. The review, the kiss. She will remember writing a review that shredded some bad poet she didn't know. She will remember skipping out of the reading early be-cause it was just that bad, and leafing through the zine that read like a sixteen-year-old about to commit suicide. She will remember writing about some lousy crap and wondering who in the hell could write that shit. She will remember walking into Bentley's, the regular café in Tucson, and getting a coffee to go late at night, she will remember sit-ting down to read and seeing some wasted girl wander through the door. She will remember staring at the sight of that girl (who was me). She will remember thinking, *who gets so wasted on a Monday night?* She will remember wanting to walk the girl home but how they instead ended up kissing behind the café and how she never saw the girl again and never got a name or anything. And then, years later, Buddy will be sitting in her living room, watching *Oprah,* and the whole story will crystallize.

Oprah will turn to me and ask me about my failings. Oprah will look at me and say, "What was all that rejection like? Before the little pink book was published?" I will look at Oprah. I will say to her, "I almost quit writing all together. I was in college, see, and got this review in the *Arizona Daily Star.* God, it was awful, I mean I don't think it's possible to get a worse review." (But of course I barely re-member this. After all, I don't dwell on such pettiness!) I'll tell Oprah how I vowed never to write another line of poetry again. "I wrote such crap!" I'll smile and say how at twenty I was washed up, how I didn't know anything about truth, so how could I write?

And Buddy will be sitting in her apartment in LA, working on some new review, watching *Oprah,* and she will suddenly see the whole story. All of it. From all those years ago. She will suddenly get it that the little pink book was written by that drunk girl she kissed be-hind the café, and that the drunk girl she kissed is the bad poet she hated.

Buddy Holly will turn up the volume and say out loud: "Holy shit! I kissed the worst poet in school!" She will remember the review and writing things like "excruciating to listen to" and "lacked essential truth." How she wrote "the writer fails to have any original insights into either herself or the world around her." And it won't stop there. She will remember telling everyone how that poet chick was such a hack, how the girl writes for shit, has no sense of self. She will remember the sophomoric verses, the self-indulgence. Buddy would have no way of knowing this would ring over and over in my ears. *No sense of self.*

But I will have no way of knowing that Buddy is actually evil review girl, that it's her sitting there in the Novel Cafe working on a review of my little pink book. And in that moment there will be a terrible clicking in the wheels of the universe, an awful mechanical screeching, like breaks slamming and hammers being thrown. But I will be oblivious to it all. I will only look at Buddy as someone I want to know. Someone who is pulling me toward her. Something about gravity. Inevitability.

Henry will pull out a chair and sit directly across from me, which will block my view of Buddy. Most unfortunate. He'll say, "I need to know when it will be done." Henry will have a panicked look that rests between his eyebrows. He will be depending on me. I will look at him. I will feel all the air punched out of me. After all the glamour of the past few months, I'll feel suddenly deflated. I will know that after the book I will write comes out, I will feel like a fraud.

I will say, "I have no idea what it's about. How to make it look like anything at all. I mean there's no plot!" I will sit on my hands, trying not to tear off my skin and Henry will look at me. For the first time, he will really see me. He will say, "You're right. Nothing happens at all. But it's like Seinfeld that way, remember Seinfeld?" I will groan and say "No, no, no, it's not like that at all." I will have horrific images of some TV sitcom turned movie-of-the-week for the book I will write. I will cry out, "It's not about a bunch of people just sitting around." He'll say, "I know, I know, but it was a plotless thing that worked. And that's your book, isn't it?" He'll say, "I'm seeing curtains pulling back. I'm seeing stages and gaudy French theaters. Think *Moulin Rouge* meets *The Secret Life of Walter Mitty*." I will think Henry went mad in my tiny attic. I will say, "What, what on earth ?!" And he will say, "Picture it." He will say, "God, I would love to pitch all this to Spielberg. Maybe he'll let me assist." Henry will go on, saying, "You're sitting at your desk, only your desk actually looks out at the sand and the ocean and the film moves outward, from this tiny place it opens up to the world. That's it. That's how it starts."

Henry won't wait for me to respond. He'll go on about his schedule and filming and that it's got to launch soon. He'll talk about possible losses by delay and the importance of the release date. He'll say it's got to be timed just right. I'll see him fantasizing about my little pink book being a big box office hit; about how it would make his future. And I'll see how, like me, he is using the book I will write to feel important.

Henry will say my little pink book will be the movie sensation of the decade. "Just wait," he'll say. "You'll see." I will think it's no coincidence that DreamWorks is the name of Spielberg's company. At the Novel Cafe Henry will not ask about the funeral because he is a person who will, by ignoring the situation, think he is looking after my feelings. He will be kind that way. Buddy Holly will get up to get a refill. She'll walk past me and pretend not to notice me. But on her table I'll see my book under a stack of papers almost out of view. There it will be. So I'll be right in guessing she's noticed me and is only pretending otherwise.

When the book I will write is published, there will be those people who pretend not to notice me, but do, and those who come up right off and say something. The latter is more honest and I'll like that, but I'll identify with the self-conscious nature of the first group, so either will be okay with me. Buddy Holly will ask the lady at the counter for another cappuccino. I'll hear her ask for whole milk and decide she must be an okay girl. I don't go in for the no-fat milk thing. I mean, what's a half-cup of milk going to do? Will I explode in an eruption of fat by drinking a half-cup of it? Buddy will turn, add extra sugar, and glance over at me talking to Henry. I will see her sizing me up. Her eyes will be narrow, but I will interpret this as serious interest. I will not be listening to Henry; I will be wondering what Buddy's real name could be.

Henry will snap his fingers in front of my face to get me to pay attention again. Who does that? I won't say anything though, because, after all, I will have indeed been ignoring him. Henry will call up Spielberg on his cell phone. He'll say, "I'm here talking with her, yeah, yeah, the pink book, I think we've got it. Can I get some time with you?" Henry will remind Spielberg that production begins in five days. And this is when Buddy will be walking back with her cappuccino and I will only be dreaming about Buddy Holly.

By two forty-five Henry will be wired and scratching himself. I will not know why he is there with me at all. My laptop will be open and we'll be running through lines. I will be trying to write new ones and check out Buddy and please Henry all at once. I will hardly write a word. Henry will suddenly proclaim: "I've got to call my wife." And like that he will walk out the door to chat. This is when Buddy will make her move. She won't fumble or stutter or do anything that one might find awkward or embarrassing. She will be entirely charming and bright.

Buddy will lean over her table and say, "Hey, how's the screenplay going? You're turning the book into a movie, huh?" And I will like it that she doesn't say, (A) "Oh you wrote the little pink book, didn't you?" or (B) "I think it's a great book." In either case I would be left only with a "Yeah, thanks" answer. So I'll say, "Yeah, it's a trip. Months ago I couldn't pay my phone bill. Can you believe it?" She'll laugh and say she can relate. Buddy and I will talk about being broke until Henry comes back. At which point I'll smile at Buddy and that will be the end of our conversation. Buddy will not remind me who she is. She will only smile and go back to what she was doing before. I will think her smile is inviting. I will take our encounter as a good sign. An omen of something to come.

Henry will pick up his now cold coffee and take a sip. He'll make a face that tells me he hates the coffee and doesn't say anything for a while. I'll look over at Buddy, who will be back to scratching her head and staring at her computer, and I'll wonder if everyone who drinks coffee scratches that much.

When Henry and I leave the café for the day, Buddy Holly will look up and nod a good-bye. We won't exchange one-liners that only mean good-bye. I'll nod back and Henry and I will walk out the door. He will be lost in thought and suddenly burst out, "We didn't get anything done. Tomorrow we've got to get cracking." I will look down at his side, and, as I'll suspect, his hand will be slightly twitching. To cover it up he'll pull out his key chain in one smooth move and hit the button that turns off his alarm. His used BMW will beep in front of me and he'll get in it and drive away, just like that.

I will retrace my steps back to the house on Bernard, but in the middle of my walking I will decide to go to the beach instead of home. No one will be at home and I will not feel like being alone. So I will walk over to the beach with my coffee to go and mill through the crowd of strangers. In the crowds at the beach, I will strangely miss my grandfather's face.

I will be walking along and thinking about ways to die. Pills. Rope. Guns. I will wonder which is the easiest way to go. A gun would seem terribly messy. Dramatic. Rope would probably hurt too much. What if I couldn't kick the chair out from under me? What if the beam I used snapped? How embarrassing. Pills will seem decent. A sort of fall-asleep-till-you-die ending. Never-never land. I will be walking toward the ocean counting out all the ways to go. In my bath with a razor. In bed with booze and pills and a bag over my head that's covered with tape. The more I will think, the more I will know that I am terribly close. Despite the book I will write I will still feel so far away from others that I won't know what else I can do.

My little pink book will float in the back of my mind the way suicide does for the desperate. It will be the thing that saves me. Only not really. It will be the object that I will hope will save me, only it won't be able to do that. It will be the book that came from desire. That's all.

The streets in Venice Beach have strange names: names like Ozone and Rose that are separated by a few streets. It make me think about the connections. Some mornings before my walk the news lady on TV will say stuff about rethinking that morning run because of the smog. On those days, when I open the door, the blue of the sky will look like any other day. I'll go to the end of Bernard and walk west on Rose until I hit the beach. All sorts of hippie cars will be parked in the lot by the water. Big leftover school buses with purple and orange flowers painted all over them. The kids who camp in them will sell bracelets and necklaces on the boardwalk, things they've made. I went through a hippie phase once back in college. Tucson is a big hippie town, but I was too uptight to be a real hippie. I wanted to plan things out.

I'll stop at the Rose Cafe at Main and Rose and get another coffee to go. There'll be no one famous, so there'll be nothing to tell my mom when she calls.

I'll take my coffee and walk to where the waves trickle out over the sand and sit down a foot from the edge of the water. I will sit there in the sand, looking west to the vague outline of the Channel Islands. I will look northish toward Zuma and run my hands over the warm sand and make lines in it as if my hands were rakes. It will strike me that the book I will write will make me famous in an invisible sort of way.

I will sit at the edge of the Pacific and watch the waves curl in on themselves and collapse. I will listen to the sea foam crackle, and I will wonder about the mail in my old mailbox in Chicago. Does the man who delivers my mail miss me? I'll take off my sneakers and socks and dig my feet under the wet sand. A few joggers will run past me in twos, like Noah's arc: fat joggers, skinny joggers, somewhere-in-between joggers. Streaks of light will run westward out over the waves as the sun sits in the sky. The beach will be covered in long afternoon shadows from the shops and homes that line the boardwalk behind it.

After the book I will write is published I will sit at the edge of the Pacific and think about my two dead brothers. I will wonder what their names were, where they were buried, if they were buried. I will wonder, yet again, why some people live through things that kill others. And the waves will roll and roll and roll.

It's there, while I'm sitting drinking my take-out coffee and listening to the sea foam and the sound of the water moving, that I will think about Buddy Holly. I will be hopelessly lost on the screenplay but Buddy will suddenly be the center of all my thoughts. I'll wonder if she's still at the café and what she is writing about. And that will lead me to wonder why everyone is concerned with my romantic status. After the book I will write is published I will still wonder if I will ever find that someone special. At the edge of the Pacific I'll watch the ocean fall out across the land and suck back into itself. Imagine Buddy Holly riding up to me on a four-foot wave.

It will not be coincidental that everything in my life is an accident. Rather, it will be this cosmic thing that I am too dense to understand. When the book I will write is published, by accident, all the accidents that follow will be (of course cause and effect) divine in their nature. Because I am too dense to get any of it, everything that happens after the book I will write is published will seem, to me, to be a series of wonderful accidents. Only, see, they won't be accidents at all. When the book I will write is written, not only people, but the universe will recognize me and suddenly my life will chug along the rhythmic line of the cosmos. After all, the book I will write is destined.

At Christmastime my little pink book will be the gift of the season. Even though I will think my little pink book is more attuned to summer. My little pink book will be stuffed in stockings and hid under trees and given as a Chanukah gift each of the eight days. Although my little pink book will not dance like sugarplums in dreams, it will set new records in sales. The publisher will send me off on another tour. The first one will have been right after its release, and I will have found it so draining that I vowed not to do another, but the publisher will insist that it helped sell my book, and I would of course want that, so I'll go along. Of course, of course. But I will tell them that I won't give out candy canes or dress up in any Christmas way. I will tell them that it's only because of the art that I am going at all. They will, in turn, roll their eyes and nod, "Yes, yes, whatever. Just do it." And I will. New York, DC. It'll start with all the biggies: San Fran, LA, San Diego, Dallas, and Vegas. In Vegas my little pink book will be featured in a display with flashing lights. Then I'll hit college towns and then I'll go home. But by this time I will not be sure if LA or Chicago is home. I will be getting used to Venice and my attic and Spielberg and the Henrys. So I will go back to LA.

My little pink book will weigh just over two pounds. Enough to make you notice it in your hands, but not enough so that it would be intimidating. The book I will write will feel like it's the right amount of weight, the same feeling as holding an apple pie. Only the pie—not the plate with the slice and some ice cream on the side. And at $13.75 it will be a steal.

When my little pink book is almost a movie, I will wake up fifteen minutes later than usual. The usual being six or quarter to. In Venice, I will wake up and throw open the fake bay window in my room. I will get up and sit down at my desk, turn on my laptop, and stare at the screen, from the screen to the sky, and back again. Over the rooftops in front of me, I won't be able to see the ocean, but I will imagine that I can, that I can smell the water and everything. In the morning in Venice I will imagine that I can smell the bits of seaweed along the shore.

Before the book I will write was published, my father admired my stick-to-it-ness. Though he secretly worried I'd end up a beggar in the streets. To be honest being a martyr had its reward. Like when my little pink book is finally a book, my father, when I will be over for dinner one Sunday night, will look over at me and smile and say, "You see, I knew you could do this." And my mom will smile too and take a bite of her well-done steak. And that night at dinner we will talk about my piles of rejections and my parents and I will laugh. My mother will remind me of that college review, and as we eat we will talk about ordinary stuff as the sun goes down behind the houses on the other side of the street. When I look up I will see the last bit of light reflecting over the roofs.

At some point I will stop lollygagging in the sand and get back up. I will pick up my coffee from the Rose Cafe and walk back over to the boardwalk in Venice. I will stop and watch the Rollerblading electric guitar player perform a rendition of Jimi Hendrix's "Hey Joe." He'll wheel in circles around the small crowd that I will seem to be a part of, strumming chords on his guitar that's plugged into an amp a few feet away. I'll hope he doesn't break his neck. On the park bench to my right, which will be toward the water, because I'm walking south, two hippie girls will be smoking pot and laughing at nothing at all. I'll hum along to the tune and wonder how much the palm reader two feet away charges. I won't believe in it, but I'll be feeling wild. Like anything can happen. After all, I will have just come from a meeting with the Henry. So I'll get my palm read. It'll cost twenty bucks.

The palm reader will be in his fifties and sit on a stolen supermarket crate with his tarot cards set up on an inverted cardboard box. I'll read the upside-down printing that tattoos the box in faint orange ink: Tropicana, Tropicana, Tropicana. The man will crack his knuckles, which I will find unusual for a fortune-teller but decide to go with the flow, and he will ask if I want my palm read or the cards. I say palm please and extend my right hand so he can see it.

I keep my laptop in my lap and let him read my hand. He'll say, "See that long line that travels down from your thumb almost to your wrist?" He'll point to the one that as it curves downward is almost in the middle of my hand. He'll say, "That's your lifeline. It's long, but is crossed by a lot of little lines," he'll say. "There's a lot of loss there. You should be careful." He'll say, "Your hand reminds me of the desert, you ever been out there?" I won't say a thing. He'll say the lines in my hands are like dried-out riverbeds. And then he'll simply shrug and say he thinks I'm in love, and he'll look up at me with some sort of look in his eye that I won't recognize, as if he wants to get as far from me as he can. Or maybe that's just my imagination. I will wonder what it is that he sees. Who it is I love. I will want to grab my money out of his hand and take it all back.

The stoned girls will be digging through their backpacks, still laughing, and the Rollerblading electric guitar playing guy will have started "Hey Joe" over again, this time in a slower version. There will be, of course, a few seagulls flying low over the breaking waves way out in front of me. I will be sitting facing the ocean and the fifty-something fortune-teller will be facing the shops. Looking up to check for any potential customers, he'll say, "You've got to go and find her. She's the one." I will wonder if he means Buddy Holly. I will be wondering about Buddy a lot. I will say, "Which line says that?" I will want to know. He'll say, "No line, it's a feeling that's all." "But what about my lines?" I'll ask. "Don't they say anything?" He'll look around at the passersby, then look at me, and he'll say in a low voice, "What do you want to know? When you're going to die? You don't want to know that, do you? Isn't that exactly what you have been trying to avoid?"

The fortune-teller will say, "I think you're afraid. There's some block there." I nod. He says, "What matters is that you *love*."

He will be looking through me and will know that I am not sure I am capable of this. He will know that I might be too self-absorbed. Is this where pink will have brought me? He will see me in that instant as I am: on the edge of this great tide, watching the Pacific swell and rise. He will know I am wondering if I can take that deep breath, if I can dive in. He will pick up my hand and wrap his fingers over mine and close my hand so that it makes a fist. He will say to me, "Walk, just walk."

I'll look at him and for a second be hopeful that he'll give back my twenty bucks, but he won't. He will slide my bill off the cardboard box and stuff it in his pants pocket. He will turn to one of the stoned girls and say, "Hey! You wanna eat?" He will leave me sitting at his empty stand. I will read the "Tropicana" inscriptions again and look out at the horizon. In the background the slowed-down version of "Hey Joe" seems like a lullaby.

SIX

I will think I'm going back because I want more coffee. This is what I'll keep telling myself. Another refill. That's all. I will walk back the same way I came. I will go to the Novel Cafe to find Buddy and I will hardly be able to stop myself.

I will be thinking about my mother's cutout brides. I will be thinking about the groom she will never see and telling her the truth. My mind will flash on the tux she will never pick out. I will know in that instant that I will never be able to give her what she wants and I'll think about the weight of truth. I will remember her whispering the word "lesbian" as if it were "cancer" between bites at dinner. I will remember her talking about her friend Betsy's daughter, and how, thank God, her daughter (meaning me) is normal. Normal. I will think about words like *disown* and *forbid* and *sinner*. I will be walking north on Main Street to Pier and each step will seem like a miracle.

Before the book I will write is published, I will be at my parents' house making tacos with my mother. We will be in the kitchen cooking together. She will be browning the meat and I will be cutting tomatoes. Out of nowhere she'll say, "You're not gay are you?" And here, I will pause. I will think, *finally, the perfect time has come. I can just say it and be done with it.* But she won't be waiting for me to confess. Instead, she'll stir the beef in the pan and say, "God, you would never believe how those homosexuals behave. I mean, thank God you aren't one. It's fine and all to like them at a distance, but I tell you, it's wrong. It's just wrong, you know, how murder is wrong. It's the same." She will not even be looking at me. She will be browning her meat, adding some salt, and while I put down the knife I will feel as if that knife has slipped into me. Into my heart. I will feel it gouge me and slice all the way down my stomach. I'll bite off a hangnail and let it bleed. She won't look up, she won't stop for a second. She'll say, "I just don't care. I know it's not PC or anything, but I simply think it's wrong. Maybe it's generational. I don't know, but I can tell you

doi:10.1300/5768_06

I'm not alone." She'll turn up the heat. She will add some onions and say, "Hand me the tomatoes will you?"

I'll suck on my bloody finger and say, "Well, what would you do if I were gay? I mean, would you disown me?" And she'll get this look, like she's just eaten moldy meat. She will say, "Don't even joke about it. I will not have it. I will never accept it." She will be really mad. She will be on the edge of yelling this. She will say, "This isn't funny, so don't even pretend with me. You're getting married. Do you hear?" She will say, "Homosexuality is a choice. That's it. So you can just choose. We have plenty of married friends who are probably gay. You remember Steve Jennings don't you? No way in hell he's straight." By now she will be talking so loud that my father has come to the kitchen to see what is the matter. But she won't miss a beat. She'll say, "So don't even joke with me, do you hear?" She will stir the onions into the beef. She will turn and ask where the hot sauce is. I will open the fridge and pull it out. I won't feel a thing. My finger won't stop bleeding and I will swear in that moment my heart will have stopped beating completely. She will be telling me everything she wants to while still cleverly avoiding the real discussion. And my father will just be looking at me. It will be one of those looks that is paralyzing. It will say to me, *I know the truth and there is nothing I can do here. I am trapped in the middle. I love you both.*

I'll say, "Don't worry, don't worry. I'm not gay. Where did you get such an idea from? God mom, I'm so sure." I will say this with my best casual tone. This will end it for the moment. I will feel terribly defeated. I will be ashamed of my cowardice. I will know that in that very moment I have hurt not only myself, but so many others. I will bite off more skin and scratch at my back. I will want to make my whole body bleed. I will be thinking about those priests who whip themselves and I will feel as if I'm biting and scratching my way to purity.

I will be at the corner of Pier and Main and I will think, *I cannot breathe.* The café will be a half block down. I will go into the health food store first, the one right there on the corner, and I will look at all the frozen foods in the freezer. Frozen edamame. Frozen tofu. I will be frozen myself, trying to separate my will from my mother's. I will know instinctively that I deserve to walk back out the door and go the next fifty yards to the Novel Cafe. I will know that I deserve to find her. But what will it mean to know I deserve love, regardless of the cost? Will I be able to sacrifice my family for my life? Because it will feel like a trade-off. I will not be convinced that I can have both. There will be no proof supporting this theory. I will think back to my nameless brothers, to how much my parents wanted me. Only I will not be at all what they wanted. I will be a total surprise. I will be their worst fear. And I will have been carrying my fear with me for too long. I will turn away from the frozen food and look at the fruit. Mangos, peaches, passion fruit.

When I walk back outside the health store I will stand at the corner of Pier and Main. I will stand with my feet together. I will look down at my shoes. Watch the traffic go by. I will look at my ragged nails and in that moment I will know for certain that I am breaking my mother's heart. And it will be inevitable. It will be without malice. It will be with the most care I can muster, but I will do it regardless.

I will turn away from the traffic and the ocean out beyond. I will turn away and start walking the half block to the café.

In total I will have walked one and a half miles in a circle to arrive there. I won't even know Buddy Holly but it won't matter. I will. I'll feel as if I do, as if everything has conspired to lead me there, to that dirty LA sidewalk. I will look at myself again, check my clothes. I will notice I am a little disheveled. Wrinkled khakis. A white T-shirt. I will look how I feel. I will stand at the edge of the door. I will stare in through the windows into the café, hoping to see Buddy Holly, hoping for a glimpse before I dive. But I won't see her.

I will walk into the doorway and feel as if I have just dived under a wave. I will feel as if the water is rushing past me, through my hair, the tips of my fingers, I will feel the riptide pull through me there in the doorway as I go inside. This sense of certainty, as if the ocean is there inside me, urging me on. It will be whispering, *This is who you are, just believe.*

Buddy will be at the end of the café, coming out of the women's restroom. She will be holding the key and looking down. I will see the outline of her glasses, her hands moving along the sides of her body. Her gait will feel familiar somehow, in synch. I will go through the door. I will walk right in.

Pink love letters. Pink scented paper. Pink forget-me-nots.

It is then that I will nearly collapse in panic. I will want to run back out the door, down the sidewalk, back to the fortune-teller and tell him he's wrong, that I'm not in love, that I don't even know this chick and I'm not gay: just the way my mother ordered. I will feel ridiculous to be so old and still holding out for approval. I will feel ridiculous that I have stayed hidden for so long just to maintain the status quo in my family. I will be momentarily furious at my mother. But I'll know it's not her fault. I'll know I have done it to myself. I'll hear some therapist in the background diagnosing the situation.

The therapist will say, "Hmmmm," and push his glasses back up to the top of the bridge of his nose. He will say, "You see, you are suffering from internalized homophobia. Do you know what that is?" I will look at him plaintively. I will say, "No, no, you're wrong! I am not a homophobe, I am a homo." He will just cross his legs and nod his disagreement. "No, my dear, you are a homophobe." And I will want to scream out. I will want to tear his glasses off him and scream, "No way, I am not! Take it back, take it back right now!" Only, in my heart, I will see he is right. I will stand there in the Novel Cafe and know that I am about to go from paralyzed homophobe to out-and-out lesbo.

And it is then that Buddy Holly will look up. Buddy Holly will be walking away from the bathroom and she will look right at me. Everything will stop. All the chatter in my head, the ambient noise in the café, everything will be quiet except her smile. Her smile will say everything that I know to be true.

That true love exists. That two bodies can find each other. That gravity exists and has already been proven to work. That it is possible, despite nuclear warheads, atomic bombs, and Agent Orange, to find this thing we call love. I will know I am getting ahead of myself, that's plain, but I will also, in that moment, know that for the first time I will be giving something a chance. I will not walk away before the door even opens. And Buddy Holly will walk right up to me.

She'll say, "I'm so glad to see you. Really," she'll say, "you have no idea." And she'll laugh this easy laugh, this laugh that is welcoming and tender. I will not feel put on the spot. I'll ask, "Are you staying for a bit? Do you want some company?" She'll just keep staring and smiling and say, "Sure, sure, come on." And she'll turn toward her table and wave me back. It will be just like that. Simple. Easy. Natural. I will put my things down and go up to the counter to order. Maybe a mocha. Something sweet and decadent. I will turn back to look at her again, because I will be uncertain as to whether or not this is real: could it be happening? And Buddy will be looking at me too, watching me stand there in line, order my coffee. So I will turn my head back quickly. I will not want to seem weird or aggressive. I will have the feeling I am fumbling with buttons, that I can't get anything to stay in my hands.

When the mocha is ready it is so hot it burns my hands, and I will think, *this is how it is out there. So hot it burns.* And I will take a sip. I will try to sip that steamy hot thing as I walk back to Buddy. She will be looking at her computer. Typing a bit. I will sit down and feel my whole body sink into the chair. But it will be a wood chair, one of those Quaker-style things that are not comfortable, so the sinking will be more of a body-chair merging, not like sinking into a couch. Buddy will reach her arm across the table. She will be holding out her hand for me to shake. She will say, "So hello." She will be staring deep in my eyes as if she can see all of me. All of it. Even the deepest, messiest things. My hand will brush against her hand, and I will feel her skin against my skin. I will say hello. I will say, "I was hoping you'd still be here. I went down to the boardwalk, I was bumming around really, but I realized I never got your name so I came back. I mean, I was hoping to get your name, that's all."

And Buddy will say, "That's all? How sad!" She will have this playful look to her. Her head cocked to one side. She will be teasing me, taunting me, daring me to say what it is I mean. I will say, "No, not really, that's not really all." Buddy will close her laptop and the clicking that it makes when it shuts will seem loud and distracting. She'll put her hands on top of the computer and say, "So what is it?" She'll seem almost annoyed, but I can't tell. Maybe it'll be nerves.

This will be my chance. The chance I was hoping for. I will be aware that my thoughts of suicide are floating way out into the distance and I will pick up my mocha, sip a bit of it. I will look out the window and look at the sky. I will see myself still standing in the doorway, just about to arrive.

And then, for no reason I can think of, I will think back to college. I will think back to that land and the picture on the cover of the book I will write. Going back to where I was such a tremendous failure. And I will imagine a bit of water. I will see bits of water falling onto the land, at first just soaking it so that the dirt turns this dark, dark color, but then the water will accumulate. It will pool into blue bits of hope. There will be so much water it will flood the entire vista. The desert will be buried in blue. I will see the picture of me change. I will be under water, but not drowning, no, just the opposite. I will see how barren it was. I will see everything that I've lost. My grandfather, my blood, my brothers. Or was it just time itself? I will see my past as if it were being swept away and all that will be left is this beautiful blue crystal water, the sky, and the clouds. And I will come to know why it is I loved the desert. It was everything I thought I needed to be: independent, solitary. I will come to see that I have been slowly dying like those wildflowers that sprout up across the desert trying to hang on after the water is gone. That I was this impenetrable wall, I just didn't know it then.

I will turn back to Buddy. I will say, "It'd be fun to hang out sometime. Would you like to come over for dinner?"

And I will know that although I have asked her out, it will be vague enough to feel safe. She will not be able to know entirely from how I said it whether or not this is a date. In fact, from what I have said, she will be thinking that I remember her. She will be thinking that I am taking a chance. But she will not know if I am interested in her romantically or just as a friend. And Buddy will whip out her little black calendar. She will thumb through the pages reviewing her plans. She will be thumbing so much I will wonder if it will be that month or the next. I will feel heartbroken in that second, seeing that I am second-tier, someone to schedule way out. Meaning: she doesn't want to see me. This is how I will feel, but then she will flip back to this week, she will look up at me and say, "How's Sunday?" Two days away. "Does Sunday work for you?" And I will say, "Yes, of course." And the screenplay will not be anywhere in my head. No deadlines, no studio, no publisher, no tour, no movie. I will be thinking only, *Sunday, this Sunday.*

SEVEN

I will be walking back along the beach boardwalk and I will be looking out at the ocean hurtling itself against the sand. I will think of the screenplay and the potential of true love. I will think of my attic on Bernard and wonder how in the world I will make dinner in that place. I won't want my landlords to be there, I will wonder if I can politely kick them out of their own home. I will wonder about drugging them. Throwing them in the trunk of their car and locking it. I will think about changing the locks for two and a half hours. I will think, *there must be a way*. The waves in the ocean will be gentle; they will be caressing the sand. The waves will be how I see it. How Buddy will touch me. Pull at me, draw me closer. But it will just be dinner. Just a first date. So I will look at my feet and keep walking. I will wander past the hippie girls selling bracelets, the hippie massage workers, the druggies lining the boardwalk. It will be a sea of tie-dyed shirts and skirts and flesh. My computer will start feeling heavy. I will stop at a bench and consider it all. The people passing, the stories I can't see.

When the book I will write is published I will marvel that red and white makes pink. That intellect and heart is a marriage of both that makes pink.

My cell phone will ring and I will know that it is a Henry. I will have just seen him a few hours ago, but he will be panicking about the screenplay, again. Five days. I won't even say hello, I'll just say, "Don't worry. I can crank it out. It's getting clearer, I swear it is." And Henry will say, "God I'm a wreck. I never work this close to deadline." He will say, "I get that it has to be this way, I understand that it's being revealed, but really this pink thing could kill me. Do you hear me?" And I will say, "I know, I know. It will be done." I'll say, "I'm going home to write as we speak." And a seagull will fly overhead. One seagull will caw in the background. It will seem symbolic even as I duck to avoid being shat on.

I will crawl up the ladder to my room. For a minute I will remember climbing up my grandfather's attic steps when I was so little. For a minute the motions will overlap in my mind and I won't distinguish between the two attics. I'll just have to trust that he's dead. That I'm safe. I'll keep climbing up. I'll set up my laptop on the desk, overlooking the Astroturf. I'll plug in the computer. A few low cumulous clouds will hang in the sky, wispy things. So thin, so barely there. I will sit down and look at the computer. I will not think of a thing. No dialogue will come to me. I'll call one of the Henrys. Henry will answer on the first ring. I'll say, "I think I need that editor's number again, that guy called Nancy." And Henry will say, "Nancy, yes, Nancy. Hold on." And Henry will give me the number and say, "Could you have waited any longer?" It will be clear this Henry has only contempt for me. But I won't care. Henry's just jealous because Spielberg will favor me. And we are all that petty in LA.

Before I call Nancy I will look around the room and wonder if it would be too forward to have Buddy up there to eat. The room will be lined with books. There will be enough space for us to both sit cross-legged on the floor, and if Buddy prefers she can always sit at the desk. After all, I can pull up the attic door and make it so that we're here in our tiny, private capsule, so that we are two bodies orbiting through LA. That is how it will feel in my attic.

I dial up Nancy. "Hello? Hello? Yeah, this is Nancy. What can I do you for?" "Nancy," I say, "It's about the pink project. You know, Spielberg's people referred me to you. Listen, how many days do you need to edit the thing once I'm done? We've got five days total. What can you do?" And Nancy will be laughing at me. Nancy will think I've lost my marbles. Nancy will say, "Usually I have two months. At least." Nancy will say, "You must really be desperate. Are you desperate or something? Or are you just one of those writers who think they don't need editing?" And I will stammer, I will say, "No, no, you don't understand. There was hardly any time to begin with. Really, hardly any at all. Spielberg had a hole is his schedule and took this thing on a whim, the entire thing has been this whirl." And Nancy will most likely be holding the phone a foot from his ear, not caring to hear any of my lame excuses. But this won't deter me. I will be full of excuses. And finally I will just say it. "I don't know how to do this. I need help." And those two sentences will have taken me forever to say. From the first time I met Spielberg, that day with the rainbow mug, to the first time in the café, going over the process with Henry, to now. I should have said it day one, but refused. Despite the book I will write, I will never be able to say, "Help, please help me I can't do this alone."

And that will remind me of Buddy and my parents and pink. And I will hold onto the phone and cry and cry and cry. Nancy will say, "It's okay, don't worry, I'm here I can help you." But Nancy will have no idea that I am not actually crying about the screenplay. While the screenplay is certainly *a* problem, it is not *the* problem. And I will not know how to tell Nancy how excruciating it feels to be helped. To be visible and asking for help. I won't know how to do it. To allow it. I will be suddenly terrified that I won't be able to go through with any of it. That it will be too unbearable to be with people. I will bite down my pinkie nail. I will take a deep breath. I will think, *one thing at a time.* I will not think about deserts or attics or drowning. I will lean over the desk and open the window.

"Just tell me what to do" I'll say. Nancy will say, "Can you get it done in three days?" He'll say, "I need forty-eight hours." And the wind will pour through the window. The wind will brush against me. My laptop will start humming to life and I will click on the Microsoft Word icon. The script will pop up. It will be there. In front of me. The pink of my past. I will think about Buddy and about Sunday. I will want to have it done by then. I'll say, "Nancy, I'll have it for you Sunday afternoon. High noon." And that will seem pertinent. The time of twenty paces and quick draws. Nancy will give me his e-mail address and say, "Just send it over when you're done. I'll take care of it from there, I'll format it, edit it, get it to Spielberg's people. Are you alright with that? Will that work?" And I will feel this flood of relief. I will stare at the words on the screen and they will suddenly appear to have an order. I will say, "Yes, of course. It's perfect."

So I will hang up the phone and go to work. I will work through the burning sunset. I will work through the night, the sunrise, another setting of the sun. The words will flow out of me. And it will be something that is happening not of my accord. Rather, I will be watching myself write this thing that seems to have a life of its own. And while the book I will write will have been written much the same way, I will think that writing is not a vocation but rather a dedication. I will think I am dedicating myself to this time, so that this thing, this conglomerate of words and symbols, can breathe. I will think I am stepping into my life. And I will hardly move from the desk at all. I will pee, get some water, make coffee, but I will not eat. I will just keep pounding at the keyboard. Let my hands create this life for me. And through it all Buddy will float in the back of my mind. Buddy will be there, waiting for me to come to her.

I will sit there at the desk by the bay window and write out the whole thing. Not just the start, but the finish too, I will let it all unfold. While I am typing I will think of my mother. I will think about the day I tell her. I am a lesbian. I will be terrified she will never talk to me again. I will not want to force another loss on her. I will not want to be her third dead baby. And that is how I will feel. As if I am. As if telling her this fact will make it come true. I will be terrified that she will never see me as I am. I will have to wait for her to see that I am the same person as I was before she knew. I will have wait for her to come to me. She will have no experience in this. No way to understand what this means. She will think it's a different world. So alien. And that will make me think about galaxies. About all life, in all places, how life is composed of the same base elements. And I will want to talk about science. That nothing is outside the laws of nature. I will want to talk about "like equations." I will want to say the feelings are all the same, the experiences are all the same. We love. We lose. We die and are buried. I will want to say that the only difference is that there will be another woman, not a man. But otherwise, my love, when I love, will be precisely the same as hers. I will sit there and write out the whole screenplay and I will run that moment through my head over and over. And I will hope that just once the ending will come out right.

I will have no way of knowing that in that precise moment Buddy is rereading the book I will write, that she is taking careful notes in the margins, that she is preparing her review for the *Los Angeles Times*. I will have no way of knowing that my past is rapidly gaining on me.

Pink. n. 1. The highest or finest example, degree. 2. A person whose political or economic views are somewhat radical. 3. Pale red. Pink. v. 1. To prick or stab. 2. To hurt or irritate as by criticism. 3. To adorn, embellish.

I will finish the screenplay at 2:30 a.m. My ass will be incredibly sore and my wrists will ache. It will officially be Sunday, the day of my date. I will e-mail the document to Nancy and will crawl over to the mattress on the floor of the attic. I won't change my clothes. I will crawl under the covers, bra and all. I will lay my head down against the pillow and it will feel terrific. All that plushness. All that support.

After the book I will write is published I will not have any dreams. I will stop dreaming altogether and at first this will perplex me. I will wake up each morning with nothing, no leftover images, no feelings of any sort. Nothing. I will simply awake from the nightly comatose ready to go. I will feel that I have been revved overnight. But there will be a part of me that will miss the nightly drama. The creepy Stephen King vampires. The unending rooms that shift as I walk. I will miss my nightly flights over Tibet. I will miss my tête-à-têtes with the Dalai Lama. All of it. But I will see why it is I no longer dream. It will be obvious enough for me to get. There will no longer be a need. Because I will be actively living out all the things I used to sleep through.

I will get up at 7:00 a.m. The sun will be glaring through the window. The attic will be filled up with that early glowing, and I will want to hop out of bed, but since it's impossible in that room I will simply roll out and carefully ease myself down the attic ladder. The house will be nearly quiet, just the sound of the owners' snoring through their door. I will go to the bathroom and turn on the light. I will stare at myself in the mirror. I will wonder about the face I see staring back at me. Sometimes it will not feel like my own, as if I am surprised that this is what I look like. Regardless of how long I carry myself around I will always be surprised at how I look, that I have a solid form. Weight and mass. Mostly I will feel out-of-body. I will stare at my eyes in the mirror. I will want to say I look like somebody famous but I don't, and I am, so it will simply be me. So I will strip off my clothes and run the shower.

Rice. Meat. Greens of some sort. Maybe bread instead of rice. Maybe fish instead of meat. Or maybe tofu and no meat at all. Maybe spaghetti. No, too messy. Swordfish. Sirloin steak. Roasted peppers on the side. I will want this dinner to be the pink of perfection. Habanera something. In the shower I'll nearly have a meltdown. As if the dinner will be all about the food. I'll think about taking Buddy Holly's glasses off. Pulling her closer. What would that feel like? Chilled dill-cucumber soup and rosemary roasted tenderloin. That'll be it. Exactly.

I won't be able to go to the funky health food store up on Main and Pier. They won't sell meat. So I'll walk all the way up to the Vons on Broadway, in Santa Monica. I will hate the Vons store. It will seem déclassé. And even though I will say I am everyday-like, ordinary, the truth will be that I'm a snob. I'll be a terrified, lonely snob and I will like fancy organic places that overcharge. After the book I will write comes out and I have some money I will take great joy in buying over-priced food.

I will be at Vons picking out greens and will decide on sautéed spinach. I will be browsing bunches of spinach and this woman next to me will be looking for the freshest bunch. She will pick up one bulk, examine it, and then put it back. Over and over. And then she will see me and say, "Oh God, you're that pink lady aren't you? Isn't that little pink book yours?" And I will nod and stuff a bunch of wet spinach into a tiny plastic bag. She will ask, "Can I have your auto-graph, please?" And this is when I will have to remember humility. "Of course, of course."

I will have two bags of groceries and be dreading the walk back. And even though everyone drives in LA I will like to walk. In fact, I will walk all over Venice and Santa Monica. It will be one of my favor-ite things. To feel the cement under my feet, to be so in my body, to watch all the people in their cars sweep past me. When I finally reach the driveway of the house on Bernard my cell phone will ring and I'll rearrange my groceries to dig out the phone and answer it. Nancy won't let me say hello, he'll burst out, "This is brilliant!" He'll say it over and over, "Brilliant! It's brilliant! By God woman this thing is in the pink!" And Nancy will talk like that, as if he had a bag full of exclamations that he tacked on to the end of everything he says. I only had a few small edits! Barely a thing at all! Changed a few words here and there! Nothing! Your job is done! And the groceries in my arms will start weighing a ton; I will put them down on the cement.

"Thank you Nancy, thank you so much." I will ask, "Nancy, do you think it will come off? I mean, it might read fine, but what about as a film?" Not movie or flick. "Do you think it will look good up there on one of those big screens? Will the audience get it?" And Nancy will say, "Don't worry, don't worry, that's Spielberg's job. And besides, you know they test these things. There will be prescreenings and surveys. The producers will make sure the audience loves it." Nancy will say, "Relax, baby. It's out of your hands now." And I will laugh that he called me baby. Baby! Its so soft-porn seventies. Pre—equal rights. I will think Nancy's lost his mind. But then it will dawn on me: *Out of my hands. You're done.* I will suddenly realize that it's really all over. The book I will write will finally be finished, the movie and all of it. What'll be left of the story? I will feel suddenly naked. I will want to run in the house and lock all the doors. "Nancy," I will say, "thanks again." I will say, "You were great, just great. See you at the premiere. I gotta go." And I will get off as soon as I can. I will sit down in the driveway among my groceries. I will lie back on the cement. Stare at the clouds overhead. Buddy Holly. Buddy Holly. Buddy Holly.

But the phone will ring again and this time it'll be Spielberg. He'll say, "Nancy just e-mailed me the final thing. It's really great and early too. Damn that pink just leaps off the page. It will be fantastic, wait till you see. So about business, you'll need to be available in case there are any rewrites, so don't take off. We'll start shooting tomorrow." Spielberg will talk and talk about the movie and I will feel as if I am on hold. But I'll know he is talking to me and I will know I am part of the conversation, so I'll keep listening. He'll say, "I think it'll be a month of shooting. I'm trying to go low budget. You know, it seems like that's part of the package. An indie for pink." He says, "Yes, I'm making an indie, isn't that funny?" And he will laugh and laugh. I will say, "That's great, really, I can't wait to see it. But hey, I've gotta go, I've got two bags of groceries that need putting away. Yeah, yeah, of course, okay, check you later." And Spielberg will hang up with the regular click of his cell.

I will lie back again for a bit. I won't feel odd at all lying in the middle of the driveway in the middle of Bernard Street. I will feel very much in the middle. I will think of scales tipping. Of the Leaning Tower of Pisa collapsing. Everything will be on its side. Topsy-turvy. I will be preparing to stand up. I will think, *Yes, yes, just that.*

EIGHT

When the first copy of my little pink book arrives in my mailbox in Chicago I will hold the book next to my heart and keep it there for a good five minutes. I will feel my heart beating through the pages. And even if I won't be able to explain my need for solitude, the book at least will stand for all that time alone: late at night in the dark, sitting in my straight-backed chair, listening to the wind rattle the windows of my apartment, staring at my computer across the room, wondering if I would ever get it right. And the book will be it. That something right. The book I will write will cost $13.75 before tax.

When James's roommate, Franke, the one who works for the publisher of my little pink book, actually reads the book I will write for the first time, she will have been dying to get her hands on something new, something fresh. Because publisher types always use those terms: fresh, new, vibrant. Which reminds me why I used to be obsessed with Stein. Everything was Stein, Stein, Stein. She had this theory of the "Continuous Present" and once wrote that "Nothing changes from generation to generation . . . except the composition in which we live and the composition in which we live makes the art which we see and hear." I guess the point is that nothing is ever new, is only re-created by new generations, but then, everyone writes that so it's funny like that.

Only my book surprises everyone. Especially James's roommate who will call me as soon as she's finished the first page—the first page alone! She'll call me up and say, "I can't believe this manuscript, where have you been published before? Do you have an agent?" And I'll laugh. I will look toward my pile of rejections that I keep in a brown paper bag under my bed and say, "Well, I've had a few publications but no, no agent." And she'll say, "As soon as I finish this, I'm taking it to my boss. How long did it take you to write?" I'll be vague. She'll think I'm aloof at first, which is okay because I'm a writer, but then, after she gets to know me, she'll think it was just nerves.

Pink
© 2007 by The Haworth Press, Inc. All rights reserved.
doi:10.1300/5768_08

I will never get used to disbelief. Critics will say things like "one dog pony" and "kitsch." But I will try to explain that it's bigger than me. When I'm with Barbara Walters, right before the movie of the book I will write is released; I will say that it's about values. About valuing. Self-love (even though I will refuse to say it is self-help). Barbara will wear a red scotch-plaid dress like the kind my grand-mother used to wear, and she will look at me with those big almond eyes. I will feel that I don't belong there, sitting next to her, pretend-ing to know things that no else does. But then, she will change the subject to my childhood because she always does that. But unlike her other guests, I will not cry.

"Yes I've had umpteen million rejections, but what writer doesn't?" I'll tell her that my secret is that I look at rejection as a form of wor-ship. "Don't laugh," I'll say. "It's true." But she will wrinkle her nose regardless, and it will let her audience know that she does not believe this. In the middle of all her questions, I'll look off at the cameraman who is staring at me through a lens and I will wonder what exactly he sees that I can't. The way the two of us sit there on two matching chairs with a fake backdrop behind us. I will wonder what it's like to spend your day staring through a camera at the things happening around you at a distance. And Barbara will refer to my book as simply the little pink book and that will make me smile.

The book I will write will be ordinary, and because of that it will be great. I once heard it said on the radio that the greatest things are the simplest and least expected. And I'll use that as my outline. The shell. And when I'm on one of my walks in Venice I'll sometimes walk down along the shoreline hoping to see shells because then I can col-lect safeguards, only Venice doesn't have many shells, only broken bits of glass, and not even sea glass.

Martha Stewart will run a special on her a.m. talk show considering the new fall color: bright pink. Martha will open the show holding her perfect cup of coffee saying, "This season it's nothing but pink." My book will cause a spike in her Neilson ratings the likes of which she hasn't yet seen. My name will be mentioned as the cause behind this, only she'll angle the issue into something about linen and summer parties and the need for the perfect napkin fold, completely missing the point. But it's Martha Stewart and my little pink book will weather her misappropriation just fine. In fact, it will be good for the book because by the time she gets around to mentioning it people will be starting lose interest in the hubbub and the Reverend Jerry Falwell will chime in and say that pink is damned. He will issue a memo saying pink is the cause of the destruction of families and the reason women are working. He will formally write out for every evangelist to read that pink is what is wrong with this entire country. And the book I will write will soar right back to number one on *The New York Times* best seller list after five months on the market. So I will secretly thank Martha Stewart and the Rev. Falwell.

My favorite thing to do will be to walk into bookstores and see if anyone is actually looking at my book. And they will be. But the reason I will do this is to remind myself that they could just as easily be reading something else. It will be hard to be humble.

Pink moving vans, pink cocktails, and pink raincoats. Pink floppy hats in the summer and pink burnt skin.

The billboard for my book will be the first sentence of page one with the word "Classic" underneath it. It will be a huge marketing success. But I will never dream it's the Great American Novel, because I do not believe in such a thing. The billboard will say everything in less than twenty words. Fortunately, there will be only one billboard of my book in Santa Monica, and it'll be up by the 3rd Street Promenade so I won't have to see it all that often. Though I will go to watch them put it up. I will not be embarrassed by my occasional bouts of pride even though I'll know it's wrong.

Austen, Carver, Chandler, Cheever, Dostoevsky, Duras, Faulkner, Fitzgerald, Flaubert, John Ford, Hemingway. Oh Fitzgerald.

Before the book I will write comes out, I will stroll the aisles of Borders. I will pick up books and stare at the covers. I'll hardly blink. I'll look at them, not seeing the books in front of me, only seeing the objects in my hands: *Pale Fire, Tender Is the Night, The Great Gatsby*. This is where I'll get stuck. There will be a lot of shuffling around me. I will see people's feet moving, hear the strange cacophony of voices, but it will feel quiet. I will look up and watch the people picking up and putting down books, reading the back cover, the first and last page, the author's bio blurb: who they were, where they lived, when they died. There'll be a faint hum that comes from the lights overhead. I'll be on the first of three floors full of books.

The first floor of Borders is literature, mystery, romance, poetry, and science fiction, as well as large-print books and magazines and new arrivals and discount books and tiny daily-saying type books. The second floor cover cooking, computers, science, and music. Non-fiction, religion, history, and kid's books are in the basement. There's a café and videos on the third floor. I'll hardly ever make it to the third floor. I'll treat the bookstore like a museum. I'll go to see a few select titles then leave as quickly as possible. Otherwise I will be trapped among the murmuring browsers and the spray of florescent lights.

In Borders everyone will talk about the book they will write while I take mental notes. One man, with a tiny goatee that makes me think of the twenties in Paris, will talk about his book by using phrases I hardly understand, such as "a new look at the metaphysical subconscious" and "not socially narcissistic but introspective nonetheless." Then I'll turn and there'll be Pasternak and Proust, and I'll wonder if they too had to open one hundred and sixty rejection envelopes. I'll wonder how far my rejections would stretch if I were to line them up? The 7-Eleven a half a block away?

My favorite section in Borders will be the poetry section because no one is ever there and for whatever reason I find that a comfort. Maybe it'll be because I'm so filled up with nerves that seeing one section to-tally neglected reminds me that they're just books. But I love poetry. I'll sit on a bench and stare at Walt Whitman and hope that osmosis works through paper and time and space, that I can pick up his se-crets. I'll sit and sit and sit but won't feel at all changed. My butt will hurt from the lacquered wood bench. I'll get up and brave the Ms of fiction.

In Borders I'm not even a writer. Just someone standing in line to buy something only to realize she doesn't have any money. It's depressing. So I stare at names on the covers of the books. Flip pages of romance novels. Flip to the back of a mystery and read the ending. Sit in a chair in the corner of the first floor and watch the escalator move people up and down and wonder what each person is reading, and if they'll ever read me.

My little pink book will not be in any fancy shape. Not like those clever pocket editions or elongated so that they stand out but don't fit right on bookshelves. The only thing clever about my book will be the pink of the cover.

The book will be bought by college students and professors alike, housewives and construction workers too. The book I will write will not discriminate. There will be romance and horror all wound up within it. Self-searching and loneliness, but certainly no self-help. I will not be a guru of the soul.

I will not profit from others' misfortunes or woes. Though, since others do have misfortune and woes, it might be that those misfortunate or woeful souls do buy my book, but the motivation will be different. It will be about kinship, not leadership. So I will never feel like I have manipulated my fans. Instead, it will be like a clear gauze of understanding between us. They will lift up the book I will write and see a bit of themselves in it. They will see that deepest part of them, the part they don't want to admit and it will all be there, laid out for everyone to see.

NINE

After the book I will write comes out, but before the movie is finished, I will worry that I am not wearing the right thing. I will always feel misplaced, as if my shirt should have been that other one, over there, the one in the laundry pile. Like if I wore shirt X rather than shirt Y my life would come out completely different. I will feel as if life is like that, about choices. And the simplest ones will sometimes feel crippling.

For example, I will not have been trying to find the Novel Cafe the first day I discovered it, long before Henry and Buddy. I will have just arrived in LA and will be lugging around my laptop. Walking every which way, going according to traffic lights. I will have been in a fog. Between time zones. At each red light I will cross the street according to which way the signs allow me to go. So I'll end up going from the boardwalk over to Pacific over to Main to Pier. It will be purely accidental, like the book and the movie and how I met my imaginary lover (I will like to say this). And I will want to stress to people in all my interviews the great mystery of free will versus destiny. I will be a strong proponent of free-destiny. Something between the two. How else do you explain things? I will think that I am bound by my predisposition to places and things, likes and dislikes, patterns of behavior. But then throw in the things I can't control: upsets, earthquakes, car wrecks. So I will have happened upon the Novel Cafe. I will have been following the laws of nature, or in this case, the laws of traffic and ended up standing right in front of the door, and I will have gone in because at that juncture my laptop will feel like it weighs a ton and I will realize I am terribly thirsty. So it'll be based in part on my own desires and preferences and in part on things outside myself: traffic lights. I will think I am terribly smart.

And I will think about that a lot. Finding the Novel Cafe and eventually Buddy Holly. I will wonder what portion of it will be based on will and what part destiny. I will wonder if it's a 60/40 thing or 50/50 or what. I will want to do the math. I will wonder about the meaning

Pink
© 2007 by The Haworth Press, Inc. All rights reserved.
doi:10.1300/5768_09

of *will* and *karma*. I will remember someone telling me that God is either everything or God is nothing. So I'll decide *will* ultimately is also a God-thing. Or karma or destiny. I will decide that perhaps I am merely having trouble with semantics.

While I am getting ready to see Buddy I will have this sense that, like the book I will write, this moment too is destined. So what I choose to wear will suddenly become this big deal. This crisis of proportion. If I wear the wrong shirt Buddy might hate me. Not dislike or disregard, but hate. It could be that powerful.

This will be the Big Day. My first date with Buddy Holly.

So for what seems like hours I will stand there naked in my apartment in front of my downstairs closet that is really a cleaning supplies closet. I will be glad the owners are gone because I will be naked and paralyzed. There will be a lot riding on these clothes. Color, style. Content and expression. Yet somewhere in the back of my mind I will know this is just a story I am telling myself. Somewhere in the back of my head, like way back in the musty section I barely ever access I will know this attack of nerves is not about clothes. I will know it's not so much about what I'm putting onto my body as much as it is being in my body. The clothes are just the makeup. The last hurrah. But I will not want to think much about this. I will prefer to focus on the superficial. I'll leaf through my shirts: yellow striped, pink, white, blue, dark blue, and light. I will choose a blue blouse because it will remind me of the ocean and that will seem right. I will want to feel those waves. I will want the reassurance of the tides, that things keep moving and changing. And jeans. Because jeans are jeans after all and don't need any explaining.

I'll preheat the oven to 375. Put the meat in a bowl with olive oil and rosemary. I'll knead it together. Add some garlic cloves. Make sure it is stuffed into the tenderloin. Wash the spinach in the sink and let it dry. Chop cucumbers and dill. I'll chop and wash and season. Put the dill, the cucumbers, and some yogurt into a blender and make it spin around and around till it's a pale green mass. I'll pour it out into a bowl. Taste it. Add some sea salt. Put it in the fridge. The oven will heat and heat.

I will start to pace. I will open the front door and pace from the driveway to the kitchen. Back and forth. I will think about choices. I will think back to before the book I will write is published. I will think about how I used people. And not just imaginary ones I made up to be my beard. I will think about the long list that is nowhere as long as my list of rejections, but is too long regardless. I will think about the men I pretended to care about. The men I used to avoid being "gay." The times I said, "Oh, yeah, I'm seeing so-and-so, don't you remember me telling you about him?" And so-and-so will have been this one-month thing. I had a four-week limit. Because after four weeks I'd be so sick of myself. I'd be disgusted. I'd be thinking that if he (meaning any of them—pick a name, any name will do) touched me again I would vomit right on him. And I will have reasons. It's not you, it's me. I will cringe as I pace over the lawn, to the edge of the driveway and back. I will walk and cringe and walk through the sea of my lies. I will think I lied as naturally as I breathed. Without remorse. Without pause. I will think that before the book I will write is published I lied whenever I opened my mouth. That my body was a lie. That my hands were liars. And through my lies I would have created my comfortable cave. My lies were the pillows I placed my head on. The plush interior lining. And I will think about alienation. Self-imposed.

Before Buddy arrives I will feel as if my heart might fall out of me. I will have this feeling of anxiety that might knock me out. I will want a drink. I will want something to blot out the terror of being seen. Because it will feel that excruciating. And I will realize that in truth it's either this or suicide, that I have been holding these things in balance, that I have been holding out the idea of suicide for years, and that it wasn't just the book I will write that floated in my mind the way suicide does for the desperate. It was me. I will realize in that moment that for all these years I preferred the idea of death to being seen. To being authentic. I preferred it to trusting anyone.

It'll be there, while I'm pacing, while I'm waiting for the oven to heat, while I'm mixing and chopping and spicing, that I realize I must give up my suicide dreams. It'll be while I am waiting for Buddy Holly to find me that I will understand what it means to surrender. In midstep I will understand the difference between will power and divinity. And it will be that dramatic. Life or death. Suicide or coming out. In that moment I will see that I'll need to do this for myself. I must act. Despite my enormous (read: ridiculous) fear. And I will know how close I was. I will know that I was keeping a bottle of sleeping pills under my pillow and that every night before I went to sleep I was holding them like a stuffed animal. I will know that it was just a matter of days before I drank them all down.

Before the book I will write is published I would have been on the edge. I will remember sitting in my cockroach-filled apartment in Chicago, flipping channels on the TV, realizing that despite the number of people I knew no one could say they knew me. I will think of all the care and tenderness I used to construct my asylum. And I will remember knowing that the time was coming, how I felt it, the strange pull toward oblivion, and how I knew that with every lie I told I was slowly cutting my wrists. I would have been that dramatic.

I will stop pacing. I will put the meat in the oven. Taste the soup again. I will worry that I used too much dill, that I don't have a desert. I will worry that I am not capable of actually loving, of actually being in the world, being a part of anything. That I won't have any idea how to be present for another human being. I will not be ashamed that I am so self-absorbed. In fact, I will feel relieved that I know it.

I will tell myself it's just this day. These few hours in front of me. I will try to reign in the time so that it will seem more immediate. So that I don't have to consider visibility on a permanent basis. I can relax into a temporary agreement.

I will give up the idea of suicide.

I will realize that Buddy Holly, or perhaps just the idea of Buddy Holly, will be my salvation. That through this thing, this potential of love, I will come to life. It will be a minute or two after I realize this that the doorbell will ring and the buzzer will sound as loud as an ambulance wailing. And I will think of those red lights swirling and screaming and wailing through the streets. I will think of bodies laying on gurneys, of all the cars pulling over, making way for the ambulance to drive past. I will think about dying and cars full of dead people. I will think of the red, red light spinning around, about the white of the ambulance, and pink. I will have this moment of horror, watching in my head, as all the blood inside me pours out through some deep and terrible hole in my neck. I will see it gush out of me as if it were filling a bathtub. I will see myself fall.

I will take a deep breath.

Open the door.

Buddy Holly will be standing outside my door wearing her funky glasses and a man's suit jacket. She will be grinning and holding a bag with green paper sticking out of it. She'll say, "I hope you didn't get desert. I brought some coconut macaroons." And although I do not usually like coconut or macaroons, later on, when we eat her desert I will think they are the best things I have ever tasted. And I will smile at her, I will open the door farther and say, "That's perfect, I forgot desert! Come in."

Buddy will walk past me then turn back to face me. She will say it smells great. My hands will be sweating. I will think every pore in my body is sweating. I will hope it is not noticeable. I will say, "The only strange thing about this place is that I share it with this married couple who don't like me to be around when they're here. So I have two suggestions." And Buddy will laugh. She will stand closer to me and say, "What? What are your two suggestions?" I will back up a step and a say, "Well, we can either eat up in my room or go out to the park around the corner. But I should warn you, either scenario has its quirks, like, the park at the end of the street is where all the drug deals go down and my room is really an attic and it's about as tiny as tiny gets." And Buddy will laugh harder. She will say, "I don't really care. You pick." So I'll vote for the attic. I'll say it's small but at least we won't have to worry about guns. I'll say, "Do you want something to drink? I've got tea and juice. That's it. I don't drink." Buddy will say tea is good. "Do you have any green tea?" I'll motion for her to come with me to the kitchen and I'll say, "Sure, sure."

In the kitchen I will pour water into the tea kettle and consider the heat. I will feel like throwing all the doors and windows wide open. I will feel as if there's no air. I'll put the kettle on the stove and look down at the floor. I'll say, "Thank you for coming. I mean, I'm so glad. God, I feel silly." And Buddy Holly will lean into the kitchen doorway; she'll be watching me closely. I won't know what she's thinking. I won't be able to know that she is wondering if she should give me a chance. I won't know that Buddy Holly is wondering whether or not it's possible that I have actually matured. I'll check on the meat. Pour myself some cranberry juice and will feel like running out the door. Buddy will say, "So how's that project with Spielberg going?" She will play it safe. And this will be a big wind hitting me. I'll say, "Oh my God, guess what? I finished. I mean I really finished the screenplay. I was so scared. I didn't have a clue how to write it. I thought it'd be simple, it's really only dialogue but it was hard. It was so hard and I was so afraid I couldn't do it."

Buddy will look at me differently then, her eyes will widen in a way I haven't seen. But I won't understand. Buddy will say, "I know what you mean." She'll say, "Writing is about the hardest thing there is, you've got to be so brutal. I mean so many people just aren't capable of being honest." She'll lean toward me and say, "Do you think you are?" And I will say I'm not sure. I will say that I lied for so long about so many things, it's hard to know if I'm capable. I will tell her that mostly it's a gamble. I will tell her that I hardly ever know what it is I am writing that it just seems to fall out of me. That it scares me. I will tell her that mostly I am scared by the things I see. I will say, "You know, I put on a good show, but in truth, I don't know anything at all. I don't know if I am capable of being honest. I don't know if I am capable of writing or saying anything true. It's what scares me the most." I'll tell her I don't know if my little pink book is a success because of the marketing campaign or because of what I wrote. I will tell her I don't have any idea whatsoever. And Buddy will be standing there, arms down at her sides, and she will look defenseless, though I won't understand why. She will look at me as if she has never seen me before.

Our conversation will become a fast lobby of words and gestures and it will pull us toward each other. With every passing sentence we will see that we are more and more alike than we could have realized. And I won't know that Buddy will be saying to herself, *I need to be careful with this one. She's delicate.* I won't know that Buddy is preparing herself for the long haul. That she is sitting there, cross-legged in my attic, accepting a future with someone who might not know how to be in a relationship, that it will require her patience. I won't know in that moment that Buddy will be praying for forgiveness, the chance to be there for me.

We will slip easily from being strangers to friends. It will be like that. We will be able to chat like people who've known each other their whole lives. And I won't even be surprised. I won't have the time to reflect on that until later, after she's gone. Buddy will grab the meat from the oven for me and I will pour the soup into bowls. I'll say, "Do you think we need something else? What about spinach? Would you like some sautéed spinach? I forgot to make it but it'll only take a second. What do you think?" And Buddy will say, "No, no, we've got plenty."

I will say "Now don't laugh at my room when we go up. I'm warning you, it's going to take two or three trips to get all this food up there." Buddy will be slicing the meat and she will say, "I promise I won't laugh. You should see the dump I live in," she'll say. "I'm sure I've got you beat." I'll say, "I wouldn't lay a bet." Buddy will take our plates and I'll take the soup. We will be able to carry only one item at a time up the ladder. It will be in that moment that I realize how impossible my room is, it will be then that I will finally feel like maybe, just maybe, I should leave my attic.

I will let Buddy climb up first. I will let her go first so that I won't have to see the expression on her face when she sees it. I will hear a big whoop, a belly laugh, and I will go up after her. She will be sitting at the desk already, looking at me as I pull myself up. She will say, "You win. You definitely have me beat, but you know, it's sort of cool. I mean I get it. It feels like a cave."

I will look out through the window beyond her. I will feel all that sky, that deep, deep blue. I will feel so light in that moment, that someone understands. Without judgment. And the two of us will sit on the floor of my attic, cross-legged, and eat the food that I made. We will be two people in this tiny cave, feeling the heat of the sun, the food, and each other. It will be exactly the way I imagine it.

Between spoonfuls of soup Buddy will clear her throat. She'll say, "You know, I thought you remembered me, but I don't think you do. I've got to clear something up." She'll say, "I hope you'll still want to finish dinner, have desert or something. But I'll understand if you don't." She'll stop for a minute. She'll just sit there and look at me. And then Buddy will tell me that she is evil review girl.

I will start crying without even meaning to. I won't even understand why it is I am crying, it will have been so long ago. So petty of me to hold on to. But I will cry all the same. I will look down into my lap and cry and cry. Buddy will race down the ladder and get me some tissue. She will come back up and hand me a piece. She will say, "It's true, I couldn't stand your work." She'll say, "I was snob. I was a poetry snob and thought I knew everything, that I thought I could say whatever I wanted however I wanted. And I did." She'll clear her throat and say, "I saw you on the *Oprah* show. That's how I put it together, that it was you I trashed back in college." Buddy will look deep into my eyes. She will grab my hands and say, "I'm so sorry. I used to hurt a lot of people with my words." Buddy will keep holding my hands and say, "I had to learn how to be gentle. I hope you'll forgive me." And I will just look at her and the tears will simply fall down my face for no reason at all that I can understand.

Buddy will say, "But you know, we did meet once in Tucson." And I will look up for a moment. Blot out the tears. I will say, "Huh? I don't remember." I'll say, "I would remember you, I'm sure, but I don't remember you at all." But then I will tell her how mostly I didn't talk to anyone, and if I did, I would lie. I would tell people half-truths or out-rageous stories about myself. I will say, "One time I even said *The New Yorker* published my poetry. Can you believe it?" I will say, "I was just that insecure. Pathetic, huh?"

Buddy will say it was at Bentley's Cafe. She will go on. "I guess it shouldn't surprise me that you don't remember. You came in and or-dered some coffee. You were slurring words and knocking over chairs. So I waited to see if you were okay. I offered to walk you home. And you just stared at me like you couldn't hear me but you said, 'Okay, let's go.' Only I had no idea you were the poet I'd just reviewed. I didn't know who you were; just some drunk girl is all I thought. So we started walking outside. I was mostly holding you up and we went around the back of the café to cut through the parking lot to your place and you stopped me. You pressed into me then. You were hang-ing all over me and you kissed me. You slurred something and then passed out right there in the parking lot. You slumped into me and I laid you down on the ground and went for help."

And I will look at her in disbelief. I will say, "I don't have any mem-ory of that. I used to black out all the time." Buddy will turn her head from me, there in the attic, and she will stare out my window. She will say, "I remember watching *Oprah* and realizing it was you, that I'd kissed you one time, years ago. Isn't that strange?"

And it will be this incredible blank. Tabula Rasa. I will have the urge to kick her out and throw a big tantrum. But I will know that she is right because I always blacked out. Because I was used to hear-ing things that I did that I didn't even know I did. I will mostly be amazed that she didn't tell me how I threw up on her or ran around screaming like a maniac. I used to scream and scream: "Stop touching me, you're hurting me." And later, when I'd come to, people used to say things like: "I think you need some help; maybe you should see a psychologist or go to a hospital for a while." And they were always dead serious. But I'd pretend that everything was fine. "I'm fine, I'm fine. I just drank too much, that's all. Get over it!"

And then I would remember how tormented I felt when I saw women I was attracted to. All that longing. It was overwhelming being so afraid. And I will wonder how it could be that Buddy is there with me, that my little pink book brought me to this, that Buddy, my biggest critic, would be my redemption. How could this be? And Buddy will look at me, ask me again, "Don't you remember anything?"

And I will say, "No. Not a thing." I will ask Buddy, "So why are you here?" And she will look at me, she will say, "I had to tell you. I mean, after I saw *Oprah* I knew I'd really crossed the line with my review. Back then I didn't care that the truth was mean. I just didn't. I didn't understand I hurt people. I had no idea what it felt like to be hurt." And as Buddy talks I will stir my cucumber soup. I will look down into the bowl and think about karma and all the lies I'd told over the years. The people I'd harmed will flash and glare in my eyes. And I will know that it's okay. I will know that she was right. That I was a lousy poet and I will tell her so. I will say, "You did me a favor. Really."

I will stir my soup and take another bite. I won't say anything for a bit. I will just sit with the feelings I have. I will sit there in the attic and think about that time. I will look up at her and say, "You know, I hated myself so much I drank every night in college. I drank until I couldn't think or hear or see. I was incapable of being honest and it showed in everything I did, but especially my work. Do you know that I still haven't even told my parents I'm gay? I'm thirty-two. I should be over this by now. I should have a house, two point five kids, a partner, a car. I should be changing diapers and shopping on the home shopping channel. Instead I am hiding away behind my little pink book."

I will look at Buddy and realize that if it wasn't for her, that I never would have written the book I will write. I never would have stopped writing all that bad poetry; I would have kept trying and trying. Instead, she set me on this path. She set my future in motion.

Even after the book I will write is published I will not know how to be truthful. I will not know what it means to be transparent. I will reveal parts of me over here and other parts over there. I will spread half-truths across the continent in different magazines and on different talk shows. After the book I will write is published I will remember being told that God is either everything or nothing. I will remember that statement but will want to make exceptions. If I insert a semicolon it will be okay for me to tell outlandish stories and bat my eyes on Tuesdays and Thursdays. And if I insert an actual colon I will be able to lie about the small things on Fridays. No, I am not picking myself to death. No I am not chewing off my fingernails every time I feel vulnerable. No I am never uncomfortable; I am always tropical, a cool and mild seventy-eight degrees. It will be hard to accept that the book I will write will not be able to save me.

And I will stare into my soup and laugh out loud. Buddy will wonder what it is that I see in my soup. Buddy will be wondering what it is I am thinking. If I am about to throw her out. I will laugh and laugh. I will look at Buddy Holly and just say, "You were totally right about me. Everything you said, everything you published. The problem isn't that you told the truth; I am the problem. I wanted to write truth but I was refusing to speak it." And it will be the first time we laugh. It will be the first honest laugh between us. I will say to her, "I am really, really sick. I mean sick in the head. Completely mad." I'll tell her it's a natural occurrence for me, like opium in Afghanistan.

Then I will want to change the conversation. I will have had enough honesty for one night. I will turn to her, say, "So how did you get here? What brought you to LA?" She'll say, "I've been here since graduation." She'll say, "I came here to write. My ex and I moved here. I met her in Tucson too. Janice Wilkens. Did you know her?" And I will shake my head, I would never have heard of a Janice Wilkens. Buddy will say, "Janice and I were together for nine years, but we didn't make it. I'm not sure whose fault it was. Probably both of ours. She was trying to come out but wouldn't and I ended up leaving because she couldn't take responsibility for herself. She couldn't live her own life." And I will turn my head from her. There will be a knot in my stomach that is both longing and dread. But Buddy won't see that, she will go on. "In truth," she'll say, "I'm sure she was relieved when I left. I was too harsh back then. I would snap things out, boss her around. I had all these opinions and just said them without thinking, without considering the impact."

Buddy will say, "It's funny, but I thought I'd be a famous poet. You know, like Plath or Sexton. But turns out I'm a lousy poet too, so I just stuck to reviews. And then I left Janice and that's been a few years now." Then Buddy will pause for a minute. She'll draw herself together, get serious. She'll say, "It was only later that I realized sometimes we have to hold things for others when they can't."

Buddy will say that again, she'll say, "It took that loss for me to realize that sometimes we have to hold space for those we love. That relationships give us that. The ability to be held when we need it. Carried."

And Buddy will look at me. She will look closely at me, as if she is trying to see whether or not I understand what she means. And I will want to, but I won't. Not entirely.

I will be nervous. I will say, "I'm not sure I understand you, but I trust that it's true." And I will realize the significance of that. I will trust her. I will suddenly be aware that my heart doesn't feel like its hefty self. It will feel strangely open, as if someone had opened a window in a sunny room. I will suddenly be aware of this strange sensation and I will be slightly alarmed. Where is my wall? Where is the safety that is usually between me and whoever I'm with? I will feel naked. I will look at Buddy talking and for no known reason at all I will simply trust her. She wouldn't have earned it. She wouldn't have done anything at all except come to dinner.

And Buddy will smile at me. She'll say, "You look different." She'll say, "You look different from when we first met in Tucson. Isn't that strange? I can't put my finger on it, but you look younger somehow." And she'll suddenly take her hand and trace my jaw and that small tender thing will feel perfect. She'll just nod her head and it will seem like she understands me. And then she'll look at me, smile, and say, "I know you're afraid you can't be honest, but I know that you can because of what you write." She'll say that the little pink book is honest.

She'll say, "When you're ready, it will happen for you and you won't even realize it."

I'll look at Buddy and say, "I don't know, maybe." I will look at her and know that because of her I will have to learn how to be honest. Not just in my writing but in person, in real life. I will have no idea if I am capable of such a thing. I will wonder if other people lie like me or if I'm insane. I won't be certain.

Buddy will say, "Turns out that I'm a pretty good critic. People believe me." And then Buddy will look at me, she'll say, "But I had to learn day-to-day temperance." She'll say, "The *Los Angeles Times* picked me up and people started buying the things I recommended. Can you believe it?" And right then I will know what is coming. I will promise myself I won't panic. The air will feel as if it's dropped ten degrees. She will say, "When I saw you in the café the other day I was actually working on your review. Can you believe it?"

And I will believe it. It will seem as if it had to be this way that there was simply no other way it could possibly unfold. That it would be about forgiveness. Of her, of myself.

When we finish eating we will load the plates and cups up onto the desk and Buddy will move over to the mattress. She will be scanning the books in my room. She will offer me a macaroon. I will take it and bite into it. It will taste wonderful in my mouth. So fresh. And then Buddy will get serious. She will look at me suddenly and say, "So why did you invite me here? I mean, not knowing who I was, what was it you wanted from me?"

I will look down at the floor. I will change from sitting cross-legged to sitting on my knees, and then I'll change back. I will take a sip of tea and Buddy will just be sitting there, starting at me, waiting for an answer. She will look completely cool. Like a rock star waving from a bus, she will just be sitting there in all her confidence and I will be spinning on the floor. I'll say, "I know I don't really know you at all. I mean, really I don't, but you see—" And here I will pause. I won't be sure I can get the words out. It'll be the last ditch hurrah, the first hurrah. But the words will be stuck in my throat. I'll take another bite of macaroon and feel the sweetness. It will give me confidence, so I will simply blurt out, "I thought you were cute and wanted to go on a date. I wanted to know if you'd have any interest in dating me."

Buddy will be chewing her macaroon. She will swallow and take a sip of tea. She will take her time answering me. She will ask, "Have you dated women?" And I will think about what that means. What my past love life was like. "Dates, yes, I've had dates. I've had plenty of dates." Drunken dates, one-night only dates. Dates I never called back. Men and women. But it was only the women I felt bad about hurting. I had elaborate reasons for not caring about the men. From "historic justice" to "they're using me too." And while I will realize how awful this sounds even just in my head, it will be the truth. Before the book I will write is published I will have felt as if I was a drive-by accident, that I was a hit-and-run specialist and that no one noticed or cared because I was invisible. But that won't be true. What will be true is the hit-and-run part and the bodies I piled up against the sidewalks before taking off. All those injured bodies I abandoned. I never was been the Good Samaritan. But this will be my chance.

And I will sit there and wonder how much I should say. I will want to be careful. I will not want to scare her off. I will feel as if this is terribly important, as if being with her will somehow feel like a critical juncture. Turn right. Be careful. Go slow. I will think about driving school and parallel parking. I will say, "Yes, yes, I've dated women, only nothing serious." And this will be drastically understating the case, but it will sound reasonable. I will not think I am lying though I will be aware of the bits of gray sneaking up. What I say will not give away the willfulness of my past. It will not reveal the injustice of my actions. My refusal to be present, to be actively involved. Buddy will have only a hint of my malignant nature. It will be like a gray-toned pink. Like pink velvet pants.

Buddy will say, "I think there's a reason we found each other." I will look at her and nod. I will let her finish while I hold my breath. She will say, "It seems like you really want to change." She will grab my hands then and hold them. She will say, "Maybe we should get to know each other; we've been strangers for long enough." She will say,

"We need to go slow." And I will not have any experience with slow. I will remember all-or-nothing scenarios. Hot or cold. Disgust or lust. It will make me think of balance and I will know in that minute that I am walking into a black hole. This giant sucking force. I will feel suddenly uncomfortable. *Balance, respect, slow.* These are not words I know. Before the book I will write is written I will only know words like *temporary, blackout,* and *mistake.* But I will stare at Buddy Holly and feel comfortable enough to risk it. I will know that this is that moment. And everything will feel very precious. It will be all about "moments," as if I should frame everything that will happen. I will want to keep a book of memories. Images and words from the night. I will want to document everything as proof that people can change; that there is this mysterious force pulling at us, nudging us out of our comfort zones, which, in truth, are not comfortable at all, but are known. Familiar.

And I will call that force *gravity.* I will think that at last gravity has found me.

I will say slow is good. I'll look at her and tell her again that I haven't told my parents. But I'm about to. "Really, they're coming here soon. I've already planned it." I will say, "It's going to be hard, but I have to." And I will suggest we go for a walk. I will say, "I'm sluggish from all this food, do you wanna go over to the beach?" And Buddy will say "Yeah, that sounds great." And even though it is unlike me to leave dirty dishes lying around, I will leave everything where it is. I will even risk bugs for Buddy. And while this might not seem like a big deal, it will be for me. I will be shaking everything up.

It will be sunset when we walk out the door. I will have planned it this way. It will be cool and breezy and we will walk toward the setting sun. It won't be cheesy at all, we will be walking down Rose Avenue past the skaters and surf rats, past the gang bangers, and we will walk along, bumping into each other, laughing, catching glimpses. And the sun will be a huge burning globe in front of us. It will be all fire. We will stop at the Rose Cafe and get coffee to go. We will walk slowly, letting it all sink in.

At the beach I will suggest we walk south, down deeper into Venice. We will see the Rollerblading guitar player and all the hippies. I will point out the fortune-teller's crate, but the fortune-teller won't be there. I will confess how I paid him twenty bucks once. I will say it was a rip off. I will tell her what he said about love. And that will feel like an enormous risk. Something new. I will feel vulnerable, but Buddy will just wrap her arm around my shoulder and we will keep walking.

We will walk down to the gym on the beach and watch the people lifting weights. I will say they look like balloon people and Buddy will laugh. She'll say it looks like if you pricked them, they would make some awful shrieking like a balloon losing its air. And I will say, "Yes, exactly that's what those muscle guys look like." But I won't talk about how they are using their bodies to hide. I won't say anything about fear or insecurity. It would be too telling. So I will instead grab her hand and start running. I will say, "Let's go to the swings."

Buddy and I will sit on the swings and look out at the ocean beyond. The muscle men will grunt in the background and we will hear the waves, the people moving and talking, the scraps of music floating. We will be floating away on the swings, back and forth, forth and back and the waves will churn and churn. In the distance the sun will be a huge red mass, and it will slip underneath the horizon, it will slip like a hand under a shirt, and the sky will be this magenta pink.

Pink lips. Pink lament. Pink hair and pink feet. Pink sand on a pink horizon. Pale pink words in a pale pink sky.

I will be pumping my legs as hard as I can, letting the swing take me higher and higher. Buddy will be low-flying and steady. I will feel wild and jump. Push myself out of the seat and glide through the air. All that force behind me, gravity tossing me up, letting my body follow the laws of nature. I will arch up and out and down. I will land standing up in the sand pit and it will feel great. I will turn around with this smile that says I really accomplished something. Only I won't know what that something is. I will just be abuzz with the rush and an upset stomach. I will feel suddenly woozy. Buddy will get out of her swing and come toward me. She will say, "Are you going to be sick? Here, sit down." And she will take my hand and lead me to the edge of the sand pit, over to a bench. She will say, "The waves are really coming in, I think they're at least five or six feet." And I will catch my breath, I will say, "Yes, I think you're right. Did you see how far I flew? It felt like miles!" Buddy will put her arm around my shoulder, she will pull me closer to her, and we will just sit there like that. Each of us leaning into the other. My world will be spinning and spinning. It will be dusk and the tourists will be leaving. I will wonder about Buddy. I will want to know everything there is, all of her. We will watch the street vendors pack up their stuff. Everyone will be taking things down, packing, bending, closing, and the two of us will sit there and watch it all unfold. I will never want to get up.

Buddy will keep her arm around me and I will just sit there, feeling her weight. Buddy will look up. She'll say, "Are you comfortable?"

TEN

The last of the sun will slip under the water. The sky will fold into dark. It will be that wonderful sort of midnight blue, a blue that will remind me of roller coasters. Ferris wheels. Pink cotton candy. And the lights along the boardwalk will burn softly. Slow shadows. Slow voices in the background. Everything will feel as if it has slipped far away from us. Buddy will pull her arm away and look at me. Deep inside me. She will say, "We should head back, don't you think?" I will want to say no, never! But I won't. Instead I will say, "Did you park on Bernard? Did you drive?" She'll say, "No, I walked. I'm just a few blocks away, over on Ozone." I'll say, "That's the street I wanted to live on. Could you imagine an address like One Ozone Place? Or maybe Two-B Ozone." Buddy will roll her eyes. She'll take my hand, and we'll walk back up the boardwalk, to Rose. West on Rose to Bernard. We won't say much, but it won't be awkward. Shuffling and bumping. The past will be falling into place. Holding hands. I will know with a baffling certainty that this is who I was waiting for.

I'll turn to her, I'll say, "Wait, just wait."

"I'm afraid of your review. You're not going to slam me again are you?" And Buddy will squeeze my hand. She'll say, "There's no reason." She'll add, "At first, when I saw *Oprah,* I was all set to do it again, really, I hate to admit it but I was. I realized you were that drunk girl and for a minute I just hated you."

Buddy will pause and step closer. Buddy will say, "You're precious, do you know that?" And that will be the first time anyone would have said something like that to me. I won't know how to respond. I will want to run but instead I'll just try to smile. I'll suck it up and say thank you.

Buddy will say it's true. She'll say, "I feel like I want to be extra careful with you. I want to write something that will show people who you are. I mean who you really are. Not that indifferent person you try to be." Buddy will say, "You do that you know. At the café you

doi:10.1300/5768_10

seemed so steely, so aloof. But that's not you at all." And she will be getting closer and closer. And I'll be salivating madly because I'm so nervous and I'll feel like I need to swallow a lake or pee. And then it will happen. This horrible tear will seep out from my eye and run down my cheek and I'll feel this sharp heat of humiliation. I will be completely defenseless. And Buddy will hug me real tight, she will pick me up and twirl me gently around, and then we'll sort of tip from the weight of us. And with that all the fetters between us will burn away. We will be two people standing very close to each other, unbound by our past.

After the book I will write is published, forgiveness may not come easy, but it will come. *Forgiveness* will be a new word in an ever-expanding personal vocabulary. The act of forgiving. Forgive. 1. a. To give up resentment of or claim to requital for <forgive an insult> b. To grant relief from payment of <forgive a debt>. 2. To cease to feel resentment against (an offender): PARDON <forgive one's enemies>. After the book I will write I will realize that forgiveness has very little to do with anyone else.

Buddy Holly will be walking away and I will stand at the edge of the driveway waving good-bye. It will be like one of those scenes at the airport, only no one is actually getting on a plane and leaving. But regardless it will be one of those touching moments where two lovers are departing, even if we aren't yet lovers. I will feel like skipping. I will feel like doing somersaults in the yard. Back handsprings.

And it is then that I will remember that my parents are coming to visit. In a week. One week. My heart will plummet, almost literally. I will plan out how I will walk with them out to the pier; take my father to see where my mother and I went last time. The three of us will retrace our steps. We will all stand there at the edge and watch the ocean swell and heave below us. And I will put them up in the same fancy hotel and my mother and I will get our haircut at the same fancy place. I will want to make sure there is order to their visit, that things seem familiar.

I will pray that my mother leaves her hatbox of picture-perfect brides back in Chicago. I will pray that both my parents have, like the press, forgotten about my imaginary lover. I will pray for some sort of grace. That there is grace. It will be sometime that week. I will come out to them. At last. After the salon perhaps. After my mother and I have perfect hair. It will not be easy. After the book I will write is published all the accolades in the world will not be enough to hold off the tsunami that will rip through our lives.

I will watch Buddy disappear around the corner. I will watch the street empty out to brick, cement, and metal cars. I will walk up the drive to the house, open the door. Everything will seem suddenly empty, terribly empty, and I will realize this is how it's been all along. I just never saw it before.

I will climb up to my attic and start bringing down the dishes, one at a time. Carefully holding on to the ladder and the dishes and making my way to the kitchen. I will fill up the sink with soap and water and clean everything off. I will wash everything slowly, carefully. With care. After the book I will write is published I will still love to do the dishes, to feel that quiet, and to see that things come clean. It is my meditation. Wash, clean, dry. And I will feel as if the cycle of dishwashing is not unlike my own life. And Buddy will float in my mind. I will see Buddy standing there with me. I will feel close to her like that, as if time and space were irrelevant. I will stand there at the sink, washing our dinner plates, and it will seem as if I can feel her heart beating.

I will go back upstairs and lie down on my mattress. Stare out the window. I will curl up on my side and watch the stars peeking through the clouds. Because that night there will actually be stars. There will be this impossible light in the distance. There will be something that I can see, but cannot reach. And I will think about those stars. That bit of light. How in all likelihood those same stars no longer exist. Because that's how it is sometimes: by the time all that light reaches us, the star itself is long gone. I will think about echoes. Shadows. Leftover things that hold meaning. I will stare up at the bits of stars, those remnants of light and wonder what it will be like when

I'm gone, if there will be some memory of me, held by someone, any-one, and if that memory will be like this light falling down on me. I will be lying in bed looking out at all that light, wondering about all the things I don't know.

Buddy will call me first thing in the morning. I will be sitting at my desk, 6:00 a.m., staring at the screen wondering what's next, and Buddy will call me up. She will say, "Get dressed. I'll meet you at the Rose Cafe in ten minutes," and she'll hang up without waiting for me to respond. Get up. Go. And I will. I will throw on my cutoffs, a T-shirt, and a button-down sweater. I will grab the old black Raleigh bike that I will keep on the side of the house and I will ride down the street to meet her. At 6:00 a.m. Venice will be quiet. There will be hardly any traffic and so the rattling of the town is low. Birds. Wind. A few passing cars. Some joggers huffing. I will hop off my bike in front of the café and leave it unlocked. I will never lock that bike and no one will ever steal it. It will be the sort of unstealable bike that I will love. Because it's ugly and old and completely worthless. Buddy will be standing outside by the door waiting for me. Her arms will be folded and she will be leaning into the building. I will hug her tight and won't want to let go.

I will know in that moment how the book I will write will not change me. I will know that the only things the book itself will change are the things that I will be able to have. Objects of affection. Distractions.

I will say to Buddy, "You know I'm supposed to be interviewed with Barbara Walters soon. It's scheduled for the night before the movie is released. I mean, if Spielberg keeps to his schedule and I can't imagine he won't. He's very schedule-driven. I guess he has to be when every moment is money. I can't imagine living that way, can you?" And Buddy will say, "Barbara Wa-was. Really? No shit! First Oprah, now Barbara Wa-was." I will tell her I am afraid to go on with Barbara. What if I have to tell her 6.5 million viewers how I used ev-erything, even my writing? What if I have to tell everyone that I'm a complete failure at life and that's why I write? And I will cry. Outside the Rose Cafe, it will be the first time that I will allow myself to actually cry in public. I will not know what the feeling is. I will not understand that I am being vulnerable. I will not realize that I am letting that happen. And Buddy will wipe my face with her sleeve and she will say, "It's okay. You're not a failure, that's a lie. You know it's a lie." And she will put her hand on my head and stroke my hair. She will be gentle like that.

After the book I will write is published and I've met my Buddy Holly, I will let her hold me when I tell her that I went through people like water. I will look up into her eyes and I will say, "Water, I tell you, water." She will say, "Come on, let's go inside. Get some coffee." She will put her arm around me and we will walk through the door together.

Buddy and I will be standing in line at the counter and I will be staring at croissants. I will be wondering if I should get strawberry or raspberry jam. I will stare at Buddy and say I went out with a lot of guys. They were my beards, I just didn't tell them. I'll tell her how I tried to will myself straight, will myself into the sort of relationship my parents wanted. She will ask, "But how did you do it? I mean, how did you let yourself be with those guys? Are you bisexual?"

We will move from the counter to a table by a window. I will look out at the street, hoping for a car to go by, something to look at. I will say, "No, I'm not bisexual." I will say, "Have you heard about people cutting themselves? How they do it to feel better? How they hurt themselves on purpose to feel some control?" I will say it's like that. It was the same. I was so busy trying to be like everyone else. I had no sense of self. I never did. And Buddy will take a sip of coffee, she will say, "So did your little pink book change all that? And I will say, "No, of course not. How could it?" I will say, "That was the saddest thing you know. I mean when the book arrived. You should have seen it. I cradled it in my arms. I thought it was my salvation. I was alone in my old crappy apartment in Chicago holding onto this thing that I thought would save me. I was convinced. But when it arrived, it was just this book. Just paper and words."

I will look at her and out the window, pick up my coffee, blow on it, take a sip. I will say there are too many words. Too many labels. I will say I want to strip all that off. Tear at the walls that keep us apart. And Buddy will reach across the table. She will reach over and touch my arm. She'll say, "We're here now." And I will smile. I will feel an ease pass through me. A new feeling, a sense of comfort. In my bones, my skin. I will feel as if there is a new geography growing inside me. As if my plate tectonics were shifting, moving, and rearranging.

I will drink some more of my coffee. I will stare and stare at Buddy. I will say, "Space." Just the word. She will look at me and not understand. But I will. I will feel this sense of infinity but I won't know how to tell Buddy. I will just look at her. I will say, "I spent so much of my life not really living it, just existing." I will say, "When I see you here, I feel this new thing that I can't explain." I will say, "I feel as if things are opening. As if there is this great opening inside me." I will say, "I know this doesn't make sense, but it's what I feel." Buddy will pause and take a sip of her coffee. She will want to be careful in what she says. She'll say, "It's hard, I know, I've gone through what you're going through. Everyone has in their own way. It's called being an adult, taking responsibility for your life. And even though we will hardly know one another, we will both know that it's true."

We will get refills and then walk out to the boardwalk. It will be close to 8:00 a.m. and the beach will be filling with its usual routine. Merchants setting up. Shop owners cleaning. Street vendors unpacking. Skate rats huddling along the boardwalk, drinking coffee, talking smack. The scene will be filled with expectation. Buddy will grab my hand and we will walk together the same route that I used to take alone.

She will say, "So tell me about Barbara Wa-was. How did that come about?" I will say I had nothing to do with it. The agents and the publishers. They do it all. I just go where I'm told. Sign what I'm supposed to sign. I follow direction, that's all. We will be holding hands and walking along the ocean's edge and I will say, "You know I've become a minor industry. It's sort of freaky." And she'll say, "Yeah, I guess it must be." She'll say, "I'm almost done with your review." I'll look at her. I'll say, "I thought you couldn't do it now. I thought it was a conflict of interest?" And she'll say, "Well, yeah, there's that but it's not like I'm the only one who's ever done this sorta thing. It happens all the time." I'll say, "I hope you went easy on me." She'll say, "I was truthful. Entirely truthful, you'll see." And then my cell phone will ring and I'll pull it out of my back pocket and answer on the third ring. I will already know who it is. I wouldn't even need caller ID to know. It's a Henry, of course. It's the first day of filming. They started at 6:00 a.m. Coincidence?

The Henry will say, "Hey, it's going, it's really going! The actors are perfect. I swear, just perfect." He'll say, "So are you planning to come to the lot? I've left your name at the guard station if you want to stop by later. Feel free." He'll say, "You might get a kick out of it." I'll ask, "Can you put my girlfriend's name down too?" He'll pause. He'll say, "Girlfriend?" I'll say, "Yeah, that's right. Didn't you know?" (Because I'll want to act like everyone just should have known all along.) He'll go, "No, I never thought about it." He'll say that makes sense. He'll tell me he'll mark both of our names in the security log and that both of us should come. We'll hang up and I'll say to Buddy, "Do you want to go see Spielberg filming?"

It will be strange to watch the book I will write become a movie. It will be strange to see so much action. So much commotion. The studio will be swirling and humming. Spielberg will be pacing and barking orders. Actors, doubles, extras. There will be a zillion people milling about, chatting, waiting their turns. And great big cameras will capture it all. Everything will be exposed. The book I will write will come to life right there before me. Before Buddy and me. I will have the fear that perhaps this is something akin to the *Bride of Frankenstein,* that Spielberg is breathing life into something that should remain dead. But that will just be my own insecurity. Buddy and I will feel as if we were five and playing at make-believe. It will be hard to resist the urge to scream out, "This is totally insane. How could this be happening to me?"

I will watch the Henrys staring at Buddy and me. They will be sizing Buddy up the way they first did me. A regular one-two. They will try to gauge the relevance of Buddy Holly. I will ask one of the many Henrys to fetch us some soda. Diet. Cold, no ice. I will want to be officious. But none of the Henrys will notice. Once I speak they will pretend I do not exist. They will hover around Spielberg and wait for him to notice them. Only the lowliest Henry will bring us our soda. This Henry is a long-limbed blond thing who looks as if she has not eaten in three years. Buddy will nudge me and say, "Do you think she'd fall over if we sneezed too close?" I'll say, "I'm not sure, we'd better not try." We stand around and feel awkward until Spielberg comes and grabs us. He calls out to one of the more important Henrys, the one who worked with me the most, to fetch us two chairs. He wants us to sit with him.

One of the Henrys will be running toward Buddy and me with a phone in his hand. He will yell out, "It's for you, it's New York." It will be my publisher, who's called to tell me all about the new marketing campaign, how they've designed a new front cover. The original simplicity of pink and the desert will be traded in for pictures of famous actors and the header: SOON TO BE A MAJOR MOTION PICTURE. When I am faxed a mock-up at the studio in LA it will make me think of French whores and Avon books but the publisher will reassure me. They will say things like, "This is what we do for all books that go to film. It's an industry standard, a marketing given." I will be swirling with fast talk and growth charts. My ears will be boggled with projected sales goals and future markets. The publisher will be talking about a DVD/book gift set. T-shirts and bumper stickers.

I will say, "But what about pink?" I will have the feeling that I am losing sight of myself that the intention of my little pink book has gone terribly awry. I will see flashes of a direct mail advertisement from Blockbuster: Pre-Order Your Very Own Copy Today! Radio stations will give away coupons for discounts on the new DVD. I will look around the studio lot and Mr. Spielberg will be barking orders, cameras will be zooming, actors will be coughing, scratching, and repeating the same lines over and over.

Buddy will wait till I'm off the phone and then she will grab my arm and pinch me. She will prick me hard and I will want to jump.

My arm will turn pink. I will say, "What gives?" And she'll say, "I figured you needed it, some kind of reality check." I will repeat the words *reality check*. And Spielberg will walk over and ask if we should order in some sushi. He will say, "I love unagi. You know, that's the eel." Buddy will wrinkle her nose. She'll say, "Ew, seafood!" And I will say, "I like the spicy tuna rolls. Can we get some spicy tuna?" Spielberg will take my order and say to Buddy, "How about teriyaki chicken?" And this will seem like a perfectly natural conversation to be having. It will seem perfectly natural that we are sitting in director's chairs with Mr. Spielberg ordering sushi on the set for the movie of the book I will write.

I will notice a female grip checking out Buddy and I will have a near heart attack. I will not know what it is I am experiencing. Jealousy. Total, blinding, maddening jealousy. Later, when I will finally admit to it, I will say it felt like someone was grinding me up in their fist, as if I was a miniature bee being crushed. My throat will close up, and my intestines will get all twisted, like everything inside is going suddenly haywire. And the grip will just keep her eyes on Buddy. The grip's eyes will watch her move across the room, follow Buddy's steps move for move. And I won't be able to think. I will want someone to knock the air out of me as if it might help. As if the air was the problem. Buddy will turn to me, with the butch grip watching, and she will notice my spastic movements, my eyes bugging slightly at the corners. She will say, "What's going on? What's the matter?" But I won't want her to know. I won't want to say it. After all, she's only known me two days. She has to think I'm perfect. Like the book. Like the movie. I will think there is no room for my imperfections. I will not understand that it is my imperfections that make me who I am. I will cough, I will say, "Oh, it's just the wasabi. I ate too much wasabi on that last piece of sushi! It's burning my mouth."

That is how it will feel. A burning that goes from my mouth to my toes. A burning that gets in my brain and blots out all other thoughts. Who is that grip? Is she cuter than me? Is she smarter than me? Will Buddy like her more than me? Will I ever be enough of any one thing to satisfy her? I will suddenly be plagued by doubt. I won't know where it came from or that it's been there all along. I won't know that I've always been a jealousy freak because I would never have actually cared that much about any one person, save my parents, but they hardly count. And I will cringe that I am not the solitary island I pretend to be. I will cringe that I am a late-blooming jealousy freak.

I will have to close my eyes. I will have to close my eyes and listen to the sounds of the movie being shot. The snap of machines. The whirl of film. Voices and voices. I will be trying to listen for the grip's voice. With my eyes closed I will wonder if she is secretly mouthing love things to Buddy. I will create a subplot in my mind. Buddy's not really interested in me. Buddy will leave me as soon as something better comes along. This will seem like a certainty. On our second date I will have decided that Buddy is going to leave me. It's only a matter of when. And, while it will be entirely unconscious, I will go about setting up an elaborate array of loyalty tests. I will be like a perfume scientist and Buddy is my experimental animal. My love rat. In that moment I will determine that Buddy will leave me under the following six circumstances: (1) If someone better comes along, (2) If someone sexier and smart and stronger and saner comes along, (3) If I get fat or too thin or don't wear the right clothes or have the wrong haircut, (4) If the movie is a flop or a success or the book I will write is burned as heresy or hailed as brilliant, (5) If an old lover comes along who's changed and grown and wants her back, and, finally, (6) If I am simply not good enough, if I am too shallow or too mean or too ugly or too mentally unfit. These will be the reasons. I will just have to wait and see which it is. And I will sit there with my eyes closed in the director's chair, playing out each of the six endings. And I will start to cry. Buddy and Spielberg will shake me on the shoulders, they will wonder if I'm having a bad dream. They will say, "Wake up, wake up. Are you okay?" And I will excuse myself from the set. I will run outside to the fresh California air, to the bits of smog hovering, and I will run until I find a small, empty space, maybe sit down on a curb or hide around some corner where studios executives will simply drive past in their golf carts and leave me unnoticed. And I will cry and cry. I will suddenly be petrified of being hurt. I will suddenly be aware that Buddy can devastate me. That I am devastatable.

And that is when it happens. Buddy comes looking for me. Buddy comes searching and searching, calling after me. "Wait, come back." On the movie studio lot my true love will find me huddled near the gutter. She will pick me up and hold me. She will wipe the tears from my cheek. She will say, "What is it? What is the matter?" And I will say, "I can't tell you now. I'm afraid. But if you give me a chance, I will tell you some day. Is that okay?" And she will hold me there as tourists drive past in tour buses, snapping photos, cracking bubbles with their gum. In the background we will hear a tour guide talking about Spielberg about *Jaws* and *E.T.* We will hear the tour guide chatting over the loudspeaker. She will be saying how she was eight when *E.T.* came out. She'll say, "I'll never forget when *E.T.* was left all alone on our planet." And with that her voice will fade into the background. And I will say, "That's it. That's what I'm afraid of. Being left all alone on this planet. Do you ever feel afraid that way?" And Buddy will just hold me. We will rock back and forth on the lot. There will be this gentle swaying of body and bone and tears. She will say, "You've got it all wrong. You've been alone this whole time. But I've found you. You're home."

And we will know that it's true. That no matter how this thing turns out, it's true.

ELEVEN

I will be counting down days until my parents arrive. It will make me think about failed rocket launches, nuclear bombs. I will keep seeing all these bodies being incinerated, flesh melting, bones falling to the ground. I will begin to think that maybe I am one of those end-of-the-world freaks. THE END IS NEAR—RUN. I will begin to think that maybe I should carry signs and starve myself, that maybe I should move into LAX and wear orange robes and beg for money, that I could be my own cult. Part Hare Krishna, part Revelations profit. I would be the Queer Nuclear Ending saint, the Moses of dykes. And I will know my mother will hate that word. I will know that she will never utter that word. Not even in reference to a water outlet. The end of days will be coming and I will mark each day off my calendar carefully in red ink. Permanent marker.

Before the end of my world as I know it I will fall madly in love. Though I will have no idea what I am in for. I will not know how hard it will be or that it will require me to be entirely present. I will feel sorry for Buddy Holly. I will not understand about inner-transformation or till death do us part. I will not understand what it means to think of others. But it will be real and it will smart like hell when I finally get it, when it is almost too late. But while I am waiting to come out to my parents and the little pink book is going celluloid it will be one of those blissful ever-after phases. For an entire week I will feel the sort of elation that I had always associated with a good buzz. Let's say 5.6 beers. Only I will be sober and actually feeling the things that I feel. I will not be telling a story about someone else's experience; it will be my own. My very own love story and I will think something must be wrong. I will not have counted on that. I will have counted on fame, on an increased sense of financial security, even Spielberg was imaginable. But love?

Love will have been one of those balked-at things. A concept for the weak. Love? Never! No, no, no is what I will have always said. "I am this fierce independent thing. I am entirely without need of others."

This is what I will have said to anyone who would listen. Meaning strangers on the streets. I will have thought that songs like "Ship of Fools" and "Why do Fools Fall in Love" use the word "fool" for emphasis, to say something keenly accurate about the action of falling in love. I mean, they call it "falling" for a reason, right? Fall and fail. Friend and fiend. I would never let on that my disinterest was actually a mask. A way to avoid myself. And no one noticed because I never let anyone close enough to see.

And that will remind me of the first reporter, the one from *The New Yorker,* when we were at the diner eating our meat and potatoes, she will lean over her plate of home fries and say, "So tell me about your love life. Tell me about love." She will say, "You must have an interesting perspective." And I will play with my fork. I will fiddle with my fork, twirling it around in a circle because I will not have a thing to say about love. I will say, "Why do you ask? The book isn't really about love, I mean, sort of, but not really" (and especially not self-love or self-help). She'll say, "But really, it is." She will go on. "One might be able to say that love is its essence, it's *joie de vivre.*" I will try to stall her. I will have to say something. I will feel my chest constricting. Caving in. I will have the sense that everything is caving in on me. "So tell me," she'll say, "what about love?" I will finally say, "Can this be off the record?" And she'll look at me with this baffled expression, one of those nose crunched, eyebrows-ruffled looks. And she'll say, "Well I guess, but I really wanted a quote for the article." And I'll say, "I don't know. I mean I don't know anything about love. I don't know what it's like to have someone wait for you. I don't know what it's like to have someone stay. To stay. I've never stayed. I'm a runner. I've invested in Nike and Adidas. I've invested serious cash." And she'll say, "So there's no one? There's never been anyone in your life?" And I'll say, "That's just it. There's been an ocean of bodies but none of them knew me. I didn't know them. I can't possibly give you a quote, but I wish I could."

And the reporter will look at me with a look I will never forget. One of those pity looks. Pity! I will be published for the first time in my life and will have everything I ever imagined I wanted, but the woman sitting across from me will look at me with the sort of pity reserved for those dying. The sort of pity that you feel when you walk by an old people's home and realize that everyone in there is about to die, that it's just this sad waiting room, that they have no one because no one wants to be reminded that they're going to die too. It will be that sort of look. And I will realize with a great deal of horror that I have confessed to the wrong person.

I will take a sip of water. I will say, "I'm sorry, but I've gotta go. Thank you for coming out to see me, thank you." And I will go out the door as quickly as I can. The reporter will not know what just happened. She will think she's said something wrong, that maybe she offended me. But I will feel this burning thing in my chest, my chest will be on fire, and I will not know what it is. Just an overwhelming need to crawl into my attic, pull up the door, pull down the drapes, and get under the covers in my bed. It will not be until the day before I come out to my parents that I will accept vulnerability.

The book I will write will make people think that I am some sort of hero. The book I will write will tell everyone how honest I am, how brutally honest and insightful I can be. It will present this pink facade to the world. And the pink of my facade will become my profile, one of those perfect, angular jaws, a long slender nose of respect. My profile will be one to envy. The book I will write will raise me to superhero status without me having to do a damn thing.

So it will be entirely a surprise that I find Buddy Holly. That Buddy exists and that she is willing to perhaps love me. I will think I know what I am doing. I will think I know how to be there for another human being, that I know what compassion is, that I can think of someone else. I will think these are easy things. *Of course I am compassionate. Of course I am thoughtful, I am one of the most thoughtful people on earth* is what I'll think. After the book I will write comes out and the movie is being made I will think that I am Mother Teresa. I will not remember she's dead.

The week before my parents arrive in LA and I plan to "come out," the little pink book will keep on being filmed. It will be a week of hot shooting stars and pink cotton candy. It will be a week for the *Book of World Records*. It will be the first week I don't try to pick half my flesh off. It will be the first week that someone calls me every day just to hear my voice. It will be the first week that I can't wait to hear that someone's voice calling me. It will be the first week that I am not a total liar as soon as I wake up. And Buddy and I will spin around Venice and Santa Monica, we will fall into this ease and grace that I will be able to assume is only the first idea of love. An inkling. A gesture. Buddy and I will spend every day together. We will go to the lot and sit with Mr. Spielberg, the Henrys, and the crew. And during the making of the film of the little pink book, Buddy Holly and I will exchange looks on the set, on the street, on the bus, in the Novel Cafe, in the grocery store, on the boardwalk at the beach, we will exchange looks and feel for each other's hands and our eyes will meet and hold. We will hold like that.

Buddy will call me up the day before my parents arrive. She will say, "Come on, crawl out of that attic, we're going to the beach." She will show up at my door holding daisies. Handpicked, from some park, probably the one at the end of my street. The roots will be showing and they will be covered in dirt. The daisies will be perfect. Buddy will be standing at my door smiling at me. Buddy will be saying everything there is to say without muttering a word.

I will blurt out, "I'm terrified." I won't even thank her for the flowers and I won't realize that she's actually waiting for me to say thank you. Instead I will launch immediately into me me me and God God God and death death death. And Buddy will hold onto the flowers and her face will drop, but I won't understand why. I won't get it that I'm being self-absorbed. It will be one day before my parents arrive and I will be totally oblivious. I will say, "Maybe I should just show them the attic. Maybe it would all make more sense with visuals. Maybe I can tell them I'm a dyke and that I've been living a lie while we're out on the boardwalk, with the Jimi Hendrix Rollerblading guy going by." I will rant on and on for a good five minutes while Buddy stands there at my doorstep staring at me like she has no idea who I am, as if the woman she's spent this whole past week with has disappeared and I am just this stand-in look-alike.

But I won't have any thought of what's going on in her mind. I won't realize that this is how I've been all week and that Buddy has felt like an aside. I won't even have one of those flashes of consciousness. I will think that by merely being in her presence I am being present. I won't know that my walls have gone up and that to her I feel a bazillion miles away. Buddy will finally interrupt me, she will lift up the daisies and say, "Do you have a vase?" And this will stop me for a moment. I will say, "Oh yeah, sorry, come in." And we will walk into the kitchen but I won't even remember to hug her or kiss her hello. I won't touch her. And Buddy will feel ambushed by some unknown entity. She will feel as if she's accidentally arrived in the mental ward at some hospital named Bellevue, or something cliché like that, something with bars and lots of white paint. Buddy will be standing in my kitchen wondering if I am capable of seeing her, of thinking about anyone other than me.

And then it will hit me, but not because of anything Buddy says or does; I will just suddenly see her in a flash of window as we are standing in the kitchen and I will notice her profile, her eyes. I will see her at last. I will put the daisies down on the counter and turn to her. I will say, "I'm sorry. I'm sorry that I'm so unfocused, that I haven't even said hello." I will grab her and hold her as tight as I can. I will not want to let go and I will be struck by the thought that it always feels like that to me, that I am terrified to let go of her, because I think that at any second she will disappear. That I will be alone again.

I will finally pull away and she will see that I am crying. She will grab my hand and say, "What is the worst thing that will happen? What is the worst thing that will happen when you tell your parents you're gay?"

And I will want to turn from her. I will want to swallow all the words. I will want to run out of the house, down the street to the ocean and dive in. I won't want to surface. But I will look at her. I will say that they might not ever talk to me again, that I am afraid I will be orphaned. And then I will pause for a minute.

I will say, "No, wait, I think I'm still lying. I'm afraid I'll be another dead baby. I will be a dead baby the same as my brothers. They died the same day they were born. And now I will be just like them. My parents will bury me." And it will feel unbearable to say any of it, to say it all. I will think the sun is burning my flesh through the windows. I will feel as if there is too much air and that it's all pushing down my throat at once. And Buddy will not understand. She won't know about my parents because I will not have told her anything yet. I will have alluded to my mother's obsession with my so-called wedding, and I will not have told her about the time making tacos. I will not want to tell anyone this. I will put the daisies in water. I will place them on the kitchen counter. I will turn to Buddy and say, "I know it sounds extreme, but you don't know."

And Buddy will say, "Your parents won't orphan you, you're their only child. They love you." And she will say it again for emphasis, "They love you." And I will say, "Yes, that's all true." I will say, "I hope it's enough." I will say that I hope love can transcend prejudice. And Buddy will narrow her eyes. She will say, "What do you mean? Are your parents big old homophobes?" And I will say, "You don't know the half of it." And Buddy will open the fridge and pour herself some water. She'll say, "It'll just take time. They'll get used to it. I mean of course it's going to surprise them at first. You've been lying to them for years. What do you expect?" And then she'll look at me and say, "But you're loved, you know that right?"

Buddy will tell me over and over that I am loved. That with time it will be okay. She will be balanced and kind and sweet but I will be thinking about graves and shovels and dirt. I will be thinking about headstones and adoptive parents. I will wonder if it's too late to be adopted at thirty-two.

Buddy will drag me out of the house but it won't change my disposition. I will be stuck, absorbed in my thoughts: desolation, isolation, Timbuktu. Buddy will take me to the beach and she will pull out a perfect picnic from her backpack. She will have thought about us. About us as an entity, but I will not understand what that means. She will have packed us chicken salad with grapes, fancy sparkly water, and chocolate-covered strawberries. All my favorite things. In a week's time Buddy will have found all this out and I will still know virtually nothing about her. I will be so obsessed with the movie and my parents and coming out that I will completely loose sight of Buddy Holly. I will eat her chicken grape salad and stare out to the sea. I will say that the way the waves are crashing is how it will be with my parents. They will crash and pull and suck back out. And Buddy will grow impatient.

After two hours of me going on and on Buddy will finally have had it. She will look at me and say, "Do you even know I'm here?" And I will lie and say, "Yes, yes of course. I just thought maybe you'd want to hear about what's going on with me." I will not know that I am making things worse. I will say it's so great to have her as a support. And Buddy will look at me and say, "Do you even know that a relationship is about two people?" And Buddy will start packing up. She will be putting everything away, brushing sand from her jeans. She will look at me and wait for me to answer, to say something. She will be hoping that I say something honest. But I will not. I will not be able to say, *You're right, I've never done this, I don't know what to do or how to be.*

I won't be able to say that I feel overwhelmed with all these feelings. With all that's going on. I won't want to say that I'm afraid of trusting. That I'm totally self-absorbed. Instead I will watch her pack up and say, "Fine, just go then." And Buddy will pause with the sparkly water in her hand. She will shake her head. She'll say, "It would be nice if you asked me how I am, what's going on in my life." And that barely open heart of mine will be closing back up faster than I can possibly account for. I won't be able to move or speak. I'll just sit there and stare at her mutely. I won't be able to say anything, even though inside me, I'll want to shout out, "Stop, stop this, I think I could love you! I do care, I do care about you, I swear!" But nothing will come out. I'll be all stopped up thinking about Liquid-Plumr.

And just like that Buddy will walk away. She will stand up, zip up her backpack, and start walking back to the boardwalk, to the crowds of hippies and yuppies and businessmen. She will blend into the people coming and going and milling. And then she will be gone. I will not be able to find Buddy Holly anywhere in my view. And I will wonder, *What just happened. How did it go so terribly wrong?*

I will turn and look at the waves. I will realize that I am sitting there alone again, like I'll have done so many times. And I will think that perhaps I am just supposed to be alone, that it was a farce of an idea to begin with. But then I will watch the ocean curl into itself and I will know that I am lying. That I just wasn't able to be honest with Buddy. And the water will crash and pull and my heart will throb and ache. I will not want to cry but it will happen regardless of my will. I will be willing myself not to cry, but the more I attempt to will it the harder and harder I'll cry. And it will feel as if something is tearing deep inside me. As if something is tearing off and falling away. And it will be strange because I will have cried more in the past few days than my entire life. I will get up and chase after Buddy Holly.

Buddy will be at the swings. The same swings from our first date. She will be swinging on a swing and staring out at the horizon. And I will know that she is there. I will know it with every sense that I have, which is very little. But it will be just enough to find Buddy.

I will walk up to her and stand at her side while she swings back and forth. I will stare at her profile. I will take a deep breath and let everything out. I will say, "I have no idea what it means to be in a relationship. You're right. I don't know what the word means. I don't know how to connect my head and heart. I'm not thoughtful. I don't know what that entails." I will reach out and stop the swing. I will grab onto the chains of her seat and make her stop. I will move to stand in front of her. I will say, "If you let me, I want to learn with you." And Buddy will say yes. She will step off the swing and into my arms and say, "I'm sorry. I shouldn't have walked away like that."

Buddy will look at me and say, "I have to stay, don't you see?" She'll say, "You're my salvation too." And with that she will hug me.

She will draw me into her and we will hold one another tightly. She'll say, "If you hadn't shown up here, I was going to go find you in another minute. I shouldn't have said those mean things, I'm still learning."

After the book I will write is published it will be my greatest critic who will love me. It will be the person who said I was fake and a hack who will come to see me as whole. Because she will have been entirely right and in our being together, she will give me the chance to transform. To be thoughtful. Giving. Present. The woman I will love will love me without boundaries or end. There will be no conditions. No contractual clauses. And because of that I will learn what it means to stay.

Buddy will look at me and bring her hand up to shade her eyes from the sun. She will say, "I'm sorry, really. Are we okay?" And I will nod my head up and down. I will say this is going to take work. And Buddy will say that neither of us is perfect. Relationships are about work. I'll saddle onto the swing next to hers and the two of us will sit there at the edge of the Pacific.

And it will not be that my lover will say to me, "Wait, just wait." In the end it will be me who has to make the effort. Me who will run and hope and pray.

TWELVE

My parents will touch down at LAX in a 747. They will arrive in a huge tin bird and I will feel like vomiting. I will be waiting by luggage to meet them. All around me will be families hugging and kissing and crying, and I will know that I am about to ruin my parents' dreams.

My parents will be hand in hand on the escalator coming down to luggage. They will both be wearing hats to block out the sun. My father will already be wearing his sunglasses and he will be smiling looking around for me. And for a brief minute I will be able to see them without them seeing me. I will see these two people in love, who will have been together for nearly forty years, who are coming to see the daughter they love. To see their great success. This is what I will think. I will watch my mother freshen her lipstick, take off her hat and smooth her hair. I will watch my father keep his hand on my mother's shoulder. And then I will wave to them. I will wave and smile and pull them toward me. At baggage claim we will look like all the other families. Nothing will be different.

My father will grab their bags and I will take them outside to where the limo is waiting for us. And my father will see through this immediately. He will say, "So you still don't have a car?" And I will say, "No, not yet. But this is sorta cool, don't you think?" And he will just shrug his shoulders and climb in. He will know that I just haven't wanted to deal with it and will therefore be disappointed. He will say, "You've got money now. You can spend it you know. You should get something nice for yourself." And my mother will click her tongue. She will say, "Now we agreed not get into this. You know she hasn't changed. She probably lives in another crappy studio that I won't even be able to get her to clean. You've seen that mess in Chicago she left." She will turn to me and say, "Do you ever plan to come back and clean it?" And my father and mother and I will be seated in the back of the limo as it pulls out into traffic. I will tell the driver to go to the Beverly Hills Hotel. I will tell him to take the scenic route so we will

Pink
© 2007 by The Haworth Press, Inc. All rights reserved.
doi:10.1300/5768_12

go over to Pacific Coast Highway and north. The driver will take the long route while we sit in the back and stare out.

My father will say, "We didn't come just for a social visit you know. Your mother and I think you need help. We're worried. I know you've got a lot going on but really, you have no idea how to take care of yourself. You're too old to keep living like a bum, and we know you are, so don't even try to lie about it." And in that moment I will want to. I will want to say I have a big fancy house on the beach. I will want to say I have a maid, 2.5 cars. I will want to say, "No, no you're wrong. I'm pampering myself." But my dad will just go on. He'll say, "I didn't raise you to be that way. You should take care of yourself. We love you; we don't know why you always treat yourself like this. Like nothing. It's disgusting to us. An insult!" And he will pull my little pink book out of his traveling bag. He will say, "And this book, what the hell is this anyway? What are you trying to tell the world that you can't tell us?"

And suddenly everything would have gone entirely wrong. This will not be the way I planned it. I will have planned a big fancy lunch at the hotel. Lobster. Radicchio. Sorbet. I will have flowers waiting for them, candy, a basket of fruit. But none of that will matter. It will all come out in the backseat of the limo as we drive along the coast.

My parents will be waiting for me to say something. I will stare at the floor, at my feet. I will start biting my fingers. My mother will slap my hand away from my mouth, she'll say, "Don't do that, it drives me crazy when you pick." I'll say, "I wanted to wait for a bit to say this, I mean, I wanted to spend some time with you guys catching up." And my father will be holding onto my little pink book. He will be waiting for some answers. My mother will be sitting all bunched up, waiting to pounce. I will think to myself, *Well, maybe they already know. Maybe they're just waiting for me to say it out loud. Maybe it will be okay.* So I will look up at them.

I will say, "Mom, Dad, I love you but—" And here my mother will interrupt me. She'll say, "Oh God, this must be bad. What have you done? What's going on?" And I'll say, "Nothing, nothing. I swear.

It's just that I haven't been able to tell you guys something for a long time and it needs to be said."

I will shift in the seat. I will cross my legs and say to myself, *Please God, please don't let me hurt them too badly.* I will say, "First off, that guy I was dating was a lie. There was no guy. I made him up. But that's not what's important." I will say, "The truth is that I'm gay. That I've been hiding it from you for all these years." And then there will be nothing.

No sound at all. The limo will be completely silent except the bits of songs from the radio playing up front and the sounds of cars all around us. And then my mother will say, "I knew it. I knew you were lying about that guy. I knew it, I knew it." And her words will be exactly what I dreaded. Sharp. She will say, "Someone must have seduced you. It's true, isn't it? Some woman seduced you. It's not you; you're not that way." Her voice will be getting louder and louder and she will go on that way. "My daughter is not gay. That is not possible. This is the stupidest mistake you've ever made. Do you hear me? God, I knew you're self-destructive, but this is too much. You are making the worst choice of your life, do you understand?"

And by now she will be screaming. By now her face will be contorted and she will be screaming in my face. My father on the other hand will be silent. And that will scare me even more.

My mother will wail at me, "God, how could you do this to me?" She'll say, "If any of my friends find out I'll be ruined, do you hear me? You are so selfish. You never think of anyone but yourself. Why? Why do you need to make this choice? It must be someone doing this to you. It has to be. Are you listening? Do you even have anything to say for yourself?"

And in the backseat of the limo I will feel as if I am getting smaller and smaller. And when my father finally speaks he will simply say, "Driver, can you please turn back around? We're going back to the airport."

My mother will cross her arms around herself. She will say, "Being gay is a choice. You should just get married and ignore it." And she will scream it again, "This is a *choice*! Don't you ever think of anyone but yourself?" She will say, "I can't believe you. Have you lied about all of your boyfriends, your whole life? Who are you? I don't understand." But she won't give me a chance to reply, she will not be interested in what I have to say. She will just keep screaming about choice and betrayal and shame. And my father will say, "Do you love us at all? Do you even care that you've just broken your mother's heart?"

I will say, "I was trying to finally be honest. I want you to know me. Who I am, really who I am inside." And I will start crying. I will try to shield my face so they won't see but my mother won't be looking, she will just keep on. She will say, "If any of my friends find out I'll be ruined. Do you understand me? No one will talk to me. It might be okay in your circle, for people your age, but no one my age approves. This goes against everything I am. How could you do this to me?"

And the airport will start to loom. Over my mother's voice I will hear the airplanes overhead. I will think this is what I get for lying for so long. This is the price. And I will wonder what it would have been like if I'd come out at as a teen. I will sit there and wonder if I would have been taken to aversion therapy. If they would have tried to brainwash my gayness out of me. My mother will just start crying and my father will put his arm around her, try to comfort her. I will be the enemy combatant. They will not know who I am. My father will roll down the backseat window and throw my little pink book out the window. He will say it deserves to be with the other trash.

My mother will finally scream, "You should never have told me! I never wanted to know this. You should have just stayed in the closet. Why couldn't you have just stayed?" She will yell and yell.

And I won't say a thing. I will have nothing to say. My mother will say again and again, "It's a choice. It's just a choice, you don't have to be this way." And the limo driver will pull up to the departures area. He will find United Airlines and will pull over to the curb. I will think about the flowers waiting for them at the hotel. I will think about the reservations I've made for the week, about taking them to the set and introducing Mr. Spielberg. I will say, "Don't go, please. Please stay." But they will be opening the doors, not looking back. My father will lead my mother away, supporting her arm to help her walk.

I will climb out of the limo after them. I will yell, "Please don't go. Not like this, please stop." But I will watch them move away from me. Go in the doors, disappear.

And in that moment I will be their third dead child. I will feel buried. I will not know what it is I am feeling except a sort of hollowness I did not know that I could feel. I will climb back inside the limo and tell the driver to take me home. Bernard Street. The attic.

Coming out to my parents will go far worse than I imagined. After the book I will write comes out, I will have imagined my own coming out to be unpleasant. I will have imagined that my parents would yell and cry. But I will not have imagined that they would leave. I will not have imagined that my mother would tell me that I should just live my life as a lie. That it's better to lie than to be a homosexual.

Buddy Holly will not be expecting me to call for two days and Mr. Spielberg will have given me a few days off. He'll have said, "Come by when you get a chance, I'd love to meet your folks." But he never will meet them and no one will be expecting me, so I will walk inside the house on Bernard, close the door, and go up to the attic. I will not be sleepy so I will sit at the desk and stare out. I will be sick to my stomach. I will think that I am going to hide for the next two days. My stomach will feel as if I had swallowed an anchor. One of those big metal ones for a yacht or a cruise ship. Something huge and metallic and weighing a ton. I will stare out the window at the sky and not even know what to think.

Pink will race through me. Pink houses, pink fences, pink forks and knives. Pink guns, pink nooses, little pink pills to sleep.

I will listen to the couple who owns the house that I live in. They will be downstairs cleaning. They will be bantering back and forth talking about some party or another. Gossiping about the different couples who will go. "So-and-so is divorcing so-and-so and did you know that so-and-so cheated on so-and-so?" I will hear snippets as I sit there and do nothing at all. The anchor in my stomach will grow. It will move up my esophagus, into my head. Down my belly to my legs. I will weigh so much I will be afraid that I will tear down the house. That the couple will sue me for the ruin of their property. So I will move out of the chair and onto my mattress. I will lie down and pull the covers up around my neck.

I will wonder if my parents will ever talk to me again. I will have this feeling, not knowing if it is right or wrong, that I will never be good enough. Never whole or acceptable. And I will start to cry. Again. And even though I am sick of crying I will pull the covers over my head and let myself go. I will think of all the things I wanted to say. "Yes, you're right, it is a choice. I am choosing to live my life. I am choosing to be happy. You're right, you're right, you're right." And I will know why it is I never told them before. Because it will have been how I already felt, regardless of anything they said: That I am worthless. I wouldn't need anything else to confirm it.

I will start to feel as if I am being smothered so I will push back the covers. I will bunch up my pillow under my head and prop myself so that I can stare out at all that blue. And when I cannot stand it anymore I will get up and find my cell phone. I will call Buddy Holly. But I won't be able to get any words out. I will just start crying as soon as I hear her voice. All the pink in the world will not be able to comfort me, but Buddy's voice will. I will be that orphan. I will be, at least temporarily, without a family. But Buddy will talk to me and say, "It's okay, it's okay, you're going to be okay. I'll be right over."

My parents will be flying over the Rockies on their way back to Chicago, and Buddy Holly will be at my door. One of my landlords will let her in and she will climb up to the attic to find me.

After the book I will write is published and I am big and famous I will feel like a huge flop. I will feel like a huge crybaby fake. I will know that I am being self-indulgent and arrogant. I will know that I am a success regardless of my parents' homophobia, regardless of whether or not they ever speak to me again. After the book I will write comes out, I will learn all about karma and the effects of lying.

Buddy will climb into bed with me and hold me. She will wrap her arms around me and we will press tightly into each other. Letting our bodies find each other. Feeling that ease come over us. Buddy will kiss my neck and rub her hand over my back. I will turn toward her and say, "I'm so glad you came. Thank you for being here, for being with me. Thank you." And I will not feel as if I can say it enough. Buddy will seem like this precious gift. She will seem like this offering from God, or whatever you want to call it. She will be this person that I will be able to love if she lets me. And Buddy will smile that same gentle smile I've come so quickly to rely on. She will clear away my tears and say, "I'm here, I'm right here with you. You are not alone." And we will fall asleep like that. Her wrapped around me. The sun falling into the room.

After a few hours my cell phone will ring and wake us up. It will be Spielberg. He'll say, "I'm sorry to bother you, I know you've got your folks and all, but I there's a problem with pink." One of the Henrys will have told him how the story was all about loneliness, rejection, and Spielberg will say, "I'm not sure how to show all that on film. The setting, the style. It's just not jelling. What do you think? Hello? Are you there?" And I will say, "Yeah, yeah, I was just asleep. Sorry."

And Spielberg, without missing a beat, will say, "Oh God you came out to them in the limo, didn't you? You couldn't wait?" And I'll say it just sort of happened. And Spielberg will say, "Hiroshima just sort of happened, but someone still dropped the bomb. Why didn't you wait?" And I will change the subject. I will say, "So what about loneliness? What do you mean?" And Spielberg will say that Henry told him pink was really about rejection but that he'd always thought it was about emptiness, and Buddy will be looking at me curiously. I will brush through her hair with my fingers and smile toward her. Spielberg will say, "I'm not sure I agree with Henry. Do you think it's about rejection or emptiness?" And I will say, "Hmmmm, I'm not sure. Pink is just pink." Spielberg's other line will cut in and he'll say, "Let me get back to you." And that will be it. He will hang up without getting a suitable answer to his question.

I will not be able to imagine my parents' flight home. I will not be able to know what it is that goes on in their minds after I tell them I'm gay. I will not know how my mother will be inconsolable over the fact that I am a lesbian. I will not know that as soon as they get in the door of their home, she will go into the guest room and pull out all the clippings of brides she's collected and burn them in the alley behind their house. I will not know that she will rampage through their basement, collecting all my childhood toys and that she will take them to the Salvation Army. I will not know that she will sell off my doll house and tiny doll furniture. But my mother will do all of this after she finds out I'm gay. She will get rid of every possible trace of a future family. She will not want to be reminded that whatever sort of family I will have, if I ever have one, will not look like hers.

I will not be able to know that my mother will cry herself to sleep for months, that my father will have to sleep in the guest room because they cannot get along. I will not know that all my mother will talk about for the first three months of learning the news is death. She will go on and on about dying about how her heart is breaking. She will burst into tears every time she is with friends and they mention their children. She will stop going out. She will not be able to look at any of her friends because she will be afraid that homosexuality is contagious. That if her daughter has it, she must be marked, and that maybe someone will see that there is something wrong with her.

But I will not know any of this. I will not know that my mother held her life's meaning in the things I did or didn't do. I will not understand that she thinks I am gay because I hate her, that I am choosing to be lesbian just to spite her. But my mother will feel these things. But mostly, she will feel as if she has somehow failed me. As if she has done something terribly wrong.

And even if I did know, I will understand that she is not trying to be mean. I will simply know that her prejudices are acceptable to everyone she knows, the way segregation was in the South, how they all felt it was okay because everyone agreed it was okay, so no one talked about things being any different. But this will not make it right.

And although it will crush me, I will have to let her suffer. I will have to let her decide to either love me or not. After my parents leave me at the Los Angeles airport, I will have to wait for them to come to me.

I will hang up the phone with Spielberg and turn back to Buddy Holly. I will say, "Spielberg was asking me what pink is about. He and one of his Henrys can't seem to agree." I'll say, "They're wondering if it's emptiness, rejection, or loneliness." I'll look at Buddy and say, "Is there even much of a difference?" And I will wonder if Spielberg is thinking of emptiness as a Buddhist concept or as simply shallow. I won't have a clue.

And just when I've finally fallen asleep the cell will ring again. The light from the neighbor's backyard security light will glare in my room and I'll get up. On the third ring I'll say, "Hello?" It'll be Spielberg again. He'll say, "I'm sorry but I can't sleep. Pink is making me nervous. There's something that's just not right." But I will know that he is simply unnerved by my parents' reaction to my news. He will think it's some sort of omen. I will get up out of bed, trying not to disturb Buddy, who is quietly snoring, and sit down in the chair at my desk and watch a daddy longlegs scurry across the window. I'll clear my throat.

I will say, "I don't think pink has anything to do with my parents. I mean, sure, on one level, but don't worry so much. You're brilliant Steven. Your movie will be beautiful." I will tell him how when the book first came out, I knew that he could do wonders with my little pink book. I'll say, "It's pink; of course it'll be perfect." He'll laugh and ask, "Did I wake you?"

I'll hold my cell phone to my ear and tell Spielberg that I was indeed asleep but it doesn't matter. I'll say, "I've always been bad at sleep. I get all these thoughts in the middle of the night, like three a.m., and I'm up and writing. So actually, it's good that you called." Spielberg will laugh and says he's the same way. He'll say, "You know, *Jaws* came to me at two ten a.m. exactly, and that's it. That's

what made me," he'll say. And this will remind me of standing on the
pier with my mother and the waves. He'll say, "It's easier to think
when no one else is awake." I'll say, "True, but I'm awake." He'll
make a noise like he's drinking something and say, "So get up. Get
thinking. At least this way I'll have some company." Spielberg will
say, "I need to find the perfect visual to make all the metaphors in
pink really work." And I'll say I didn't realize there were metaphors in
my little pink book. I'll say I thought it was pretty straightforward.

The neighbor's backyard security light will be a terrible shade of
yellow. It will glare in my eyes and make me think of prison breaks
and the alleged crack house on the other side of Rose, two blocks
down. Spielberg will say, "I want to go check on my kids." He'll say
good night and leave me staring out the window into the backyard
that is filled with Astroturf. The Astroturf in my neighbor's yard will
be yellow-green like my old Crayola crayon. In the middle of night
the plastic will glisten like snow, only it'll be a green glowing glisten,
not a white one.

After Spielberg and I hang up I will look out my fake bay window
to see if there are any stars, but there will be too many clouds and I
won't even find the moon. It is in that moment I will think back to
Tucson and the desert. Hiking through Cochise Stronghold, the rock
garden where I hid after Buddy's review. And I will look over at
Buddy asleep in my bed and feel grateful for it all.

After three hours I'll know I won't fall back asleep, so I will scrib-
ble a note for Buddy, climb down the ladder, and go for a run. I'll pull
out my sweats, change from my pajamas, throw on my sneakers, and
go. I'll figure I will stretch at the beach. The air will have that new-
day chill and my muscles will feel useless. I will run slow and feel the
weight of my body. I will think about my little pink book becoming a
movie. About my parents. I will wonder what it will be like to see it in
celluloid, on the big screen. Will I go to the premiere in a limo with
Spielberg and his wife? Will I even be invited? Will my parents ever
see it? As I run west on Rose I will think about pink coffee mugs and
pink sweatshirts that will be sold as movie merchandize. When I hit
the bike trail along the beach I will run north toward Santa Monica.

Since I'll be a block south of Santa Monica, I will like to run north because going into another area will make me feel like I've run that much farther. Almost all of the joggers who will be out, and there won't be many at 5:00 a.m., will pass me, except one old lady in her seventies who will be actually speed walking, not running. That is how slow I will run.

I will run underneath the pier through a makeshift tunnel and keep plodding north, following the curvy sidewalk that smothers the sand. The sun will be nowhere in sight, but I will see the moon: a tiny sliver beneath the layer of smog that lines the western horizon. Everything will be quiet at 5:00 a.m. Even the waves will be gentler than usual. I will feel my face turning bright red from being dehydrated. I'll decide to walk for a bit. It won't take long for the seventy-year-old speed walker to catch up and pass me. But it won't make me think of how out of shape I am, instead it will make me think about my next book. All the hours of sitting alone.

I will be walking and thinking about the second book I will write when Richard Gere will suddenly run past me. My mother would have been thrilled to hear it: two sightings of one star. I could just hear her asking, "Oh Gere, he's a Buddhist, right? What's a Buddhist anyway?" I would have said, "They sit around a lot and think about nothing." And my mother may have laughed and said, "You're the perfect Buddhist. Too bad you're Episcopalian."

I will stop running and walk south back to Venice and hope it's getting late enough so that a coffee shop will be open. I will think about Buddy sleeping in my bed. I'll stop at a pay phone and decide to call Spielberg regardless of the time. It'll be about quarter to seven and Spielberg will be sound asleep. His wife, Kate, will say, "Hold on, I'll wake him." The first thing Spielberg will say is, "What time is it?" I'll shrug, though he won't know that, and say, "Listen, I don't think it's about rejection. Not exactly." And he'll say, "I knew Henry was wrong. Crap," he'll say, "come over in an hour. I'll have coffee." So I'll hop a bus to Beverly Hills where he lives.

When I knock on Spielberg's door he'll still be in his robe. His slippers will look like toy rabbits. He'll say, "My wife gave them to me— don't say anything." And since he hasn't yet had his coffee, I'll ignore his slippers. Spielberg, who will be walking toward his kitchen, will turn and stare at me, and say, "What's with you and all that solitary stuff anyway?" I will tell him, "I don't know, it's a long story." Spielberg will say, "Well, get over it. I've got a movie to make."

My little pink book will rest on Spielberg's fireplace mantle. Spielberg will leave it there to remember the project at all times. It will be his anthem. Hot. Hip. New. Wow. He will be obsessed with pink and the book I will write will fade from Ferris wheel pink to a soft-serve, strawberry ice cream.

Spielberg will say, "Okay, I need a frame for all this, maybe some overarching image. It's too loosey-goosey and my actors are getting annoyed. And I can't decide if it should be in a city or a desert so I've just been shooting it piecemeal. You know, all the internal dialogue stuff." And I will ask for a pen and try to write an outline of major points. Only I won't. Instead I will cry and his wife will run into the room with a hankie.

My little pink book will not win the Nobel Prize, but this will not surprise me. After all, it is pink and I'm only thirty-two and while I will dream of being the youngest Nobel winner ever, the little pink book will not be the book that wins it. Back when my mother and I were will cleaning out my grandfather's house, after he's died, I will find a copy of my little pink book next to his dentures on the back of the toilet in his bathroom. His teeth will be there in a round, clear glass. Slightly yellowed. His teeth will be magnified in the glass, and will cast a shadow across the pink of my book. My little pink book will be on the backs of toilets across the nation. And even though the book I will write will not win any fancy prizes, I will know that people have at least read my book by where they keep it.

Pink lipstick, pink bookmarks, pink sunglasses. Pink laptop computers, pink beach chairs. Pink Rollerblades, pink tequila sunrises. Pink stationary with pink envelopes and stamps with a hint of pink.

Spielberg's wife, Kate, will gently hand me the hankie and I will blow my nose even though I am usually too self-conscious to blow it in front of people. I will be wiping my eyes with my sleeves and Mr. Spielberg and his wife, Ms. Capshaw, will be sitting across from me on their love seat, staring and staring. Spielberg will say things like, "Don't worry. Your parents will come around. We always do. They love you dearly. I know it." And they will both nod toward me, urging me on.

And that's when Spielberg will leap up to exclaim, "Pink has nothing to do with emptiness or rejection at all! It's a lie." He'll turn to me and laugh, he'll say, "You're a total liar!" He'll say, "The only truth about pink being empty is that it's as empty as you were." And then he will hug me. He will grab me and hold me tight so that I can hardly breathe. He'll turn toward his wife, kiss her cheek, and say "Kate, pink is just pink! That's it exactly." Spielberg will look at me and say, "Pink is what happened when you choose to be true. That's it. It's the thing that comes from love." He will look up at their ceiling (which has no cracks) and laugh and laugh. He'll look at his wife, then me, and say it's a love story. "Damn it, after all this, I'm filming a fucking love story. I've got to get hold of my assistant."

And it's then I will know that he is a director before everything. He can see through things. And I will know it doesn't even matter if my parents accept me or not. Because I am the child who lived. Not my brothers. Just me.

Spielberg will clap. He will clap and clap and clap. Spielberg will say, "You're insane. Brilliantly insane." He'll say, "You know, that book you wrote is a trilogy. I can see it." He picks up his coffee, make sure his robe is tied tight, and says, "I can see it." He'll say it really slow. *Seeee it.* And his wife will ask if I'd like more coffee. She'll say it's good for the nerves. And I will think, for an actress, she is really sweet.

Spielberg will get on his cell, talking with all the Henrys and the studio. I'll thank Kate for the coffee and apologize for making her get up so early. I'll make my exit as gracefully as I can and find the bus back home. I'll hunker down in the seat. A love story? I will be confused but I'll try not to think about it too much. I will be thinking mostly about Buddy Holly, about how much I miss her, about how I suddenly want to see her so badly that I can barely think of anything else. I will think about the way she smells, the faint musk at her neck. I will think about love and wonder what it is. I will think about my parents and hope one day to be able to introduce Buddy. I will want so badly for them to meet. But that will be a long way off, if ever. I won't know. I will just sit looking out at the LA buildings swoosh past as the bus goes chugging along. Thinking, *maybe, just maybe.* And the bus will speed past all the dirt, kicking it up. All those tiny grains lifting and falling and lifting and falling. Changing the landscape. Changing it all.

Pink vulture. Pink rattler. Pink prickly pear. Pink wildflowers in the pink, pink sun.

THIRTEEN

It'll be the day before the movie of my little pink book comes out that I'm on the *Barbara Walters Special*. It's Robert Redford, Bill Gates, and me. An odd concoction of people, but my interview will air last and that will seem special. Since it'll have been almost a year from when my book was published, I will be accustomed to makeup people and the folks from wardrobe clucking their tongues at my clothing. I will wear gray to the Barbara Walters show: gray jeans, gray button-down sweater, with a white T-shirt underneath. And even though gray will be the hot new black I will still get the clucks. I will think I'm doomed to clucking assistants.

When I get to the set I'll be eating a McDonald's sundae and Barbara's scheduler will rush up to me and grab me by the shoulders and lead me to the dressing room without even saying hello. And I will wonder how she knows I'm me, but I will go with her regardless.

In the dressing room there will be a basket of fresh fruit with bottles of sparkling water. I'll dump the melted sundae and grab a pear. The makeup lady will follow me in with her assistant and say, "Oh, the natural look for this one, only with extra pancake first. Don't forget her eyes—they're so small we'll need to work on that." They will not stop touching my face and my hair as they swirl around me.

The commotion will make me dizzy, so I'll take a bite of the pear and ask if I can sit. The makeup lady and her assistant will laugh and say, "Do whatever." It'll be clear to me that to them I am small potatoes. There'll be such a flurry of words and gestures between them and the producer who is running around that I will keep standing there. I will be afraid to move. Someone will come in and measure me. Wardrobe will want me in Levi's jeans because someone worked out a deal with sponsorship. I'll say, "Levi's don't fit me, it's a hip thing, a thigh thing. My ass looks huge." But no one will listen. I won't see Barbara anywhere.

Pink
© 2007 by The Haworth Press, Inc. All rights reserved.
doi:10.1300/5768_13

Robert Redford will be the first interview that airs the night I'm on with Barbara Walters. But I won't watch. Instead I'll buy a video and use my landlords' VCR to tape it. I will ask Buddy to come over and watch it with me. She will laugh at me but will come anyway. She will say, "Why didn't you watch the other night when it was on?" I will say I was chicken. I will say, "If you knew what I said to her, you wouldn't watch it either." Buddy will show up with Thai food and I will pop the tape in. I will say, "Okay, but promise you won't laugh."

Buddy and I will watch Robert tell Barbara all about his ranch in Montana or Utah or one of those big empty states and I will figure that if he likes rustic, he would go for my place in Chicago, or even my attic. But then I will wonder if my places are actually rustic or just falling apart. I won't be sure. Of course I will not have seen Mr. Redford when I was there at her studio. No one will have been there for the taping except me, wardrobe, and her million and one helpers. I'll fast-forward through most of his interview, and Gates won't say anything we don't already know, so I'll fast forward through him too. Then there'll be me. After all their fuss, wardrobe will have finally agreed that indeed Levi's make me look fat. "Au natural." They'll eventually say, "You should be simple, like your book." Wardrobe will have made me wear some stupid flowy white dress that made me look like one of those stoned hippie chicks in Venice. And Buddy will laugh as soon as she sees me. She will say, "What did they do to you?" I'll say, "I know, I know, I was so thrown by wardrobe I couldn't think." And Buddy will just keep laughing.

I will decide I like the way Barbara introduced me. First there's a shot of my old apartment building, in Chicago, that'll show the window where I used to sit and stare out. It will strike me as modestly nostalgic. She'll do a voice-over that will give my now-familiar history. Then there'll be a shot of the inside of my apartment, it'll show the tiny front room, the cracks in the ceiling, everything. Then it will switch to me walking along the boardwalk in Venice Beach. Spielberg will have asked her if they could get a shot of something that encapsulates my life post-publication. Something to hype the movie. Barbara will say, "It's a simple life for a simple girl." And then the scene will go to the two of us there in the studio that's made to look like someone's living room. Perhaps mine. None of her viewers will know how far from reality the set really is. Barbara will be in the red plaid like one of my grandmother's old dresses. She will look sensible.

Buddy will scoot closer to me on the couch and turn up the volume with the remote. The couple who owns the house will come home and say they want to watch the news. They will try to kick us out but Buddy will say, "No, no, you've gotta see this. She's on Barbara Walters." And with that, Buddy will have blown my identity. My landlords won't know that I'm the author of that little pink book they keep in their bathroom. They will not have any idea. They will turn to me and stare at me like they've just seen an alien. They will suddenly gush. Buddy will look at me and understand just how deep my hiding goes. She will say, "You know I am going to love you. People are going to love you."

My landlords in the meanwhile will run to the bathroom and grab the book off the back of the toilet and ask me to autograph it. As I am signing my name, Buddy will turn the tape back on and we will all settle down to watch. I will think wardrobe was trying to make me look ethereal with the dress, but that it failed miserably. I look like I'm wearing someone else's dress that doesn't quite fit.

Barbara will start by asking the biggest thing that's changed since the book I will write has come out. I will keep it simple. I'll say, "Money." Pause for a second, and then add, "Well, I mean having it. That's new." She'll say, "Of course that's expected, but tell me, your little pink book, how did it feel?" And then they'll do the dreaded zoom-in shot on my face, and I'll see myself pause and shift in the chair. I'll see myself cross and recross my legs. I'll say, "Remember the first time the tooth fairy left you a quarter? How you were so excited but then also sad because your tooth was suddenly gone? That's how it feels." Barbara will scoot forward a bit, she'll ask, "You were sad?" I see myself trying to explain that it's not sad, that's not the right word. "No, no, it's more like how the tooth was yours, all yours, and then it was gone. It's the same with the book."

She'll ask, "Then why publish it? If you're going to feel sad, why bother at all?" I will see that she is mildly annoyed with me. I'll watch our bodies put distance between us, Barbara will lean way back. I'll see myself keep shifting in my chair. I'll say, "Barbara, let me start over. What I mean is that you work so hard at a thing, all those hours staring at a bunch of letters, trying to find an order, some kind of sense. And then all the rejections that keep pouring in. In the end, the work is all I have." But here, I will see myself getting lost in thought. I will not be making sense and I'll cringe for myself. On national TV I'll look like a fool.

I'll grab the remote out of Buddy's hands, snap it off, and say "This is crap. Forget it. I'm going to bed." And Buddy and the married couple who's house I live in will look at me as I am having a fit. Buddy at least will know I feel overexposed. I won't even let them watch far enough to see when I talk about rejection being a form of worship. I'll pop out the video. Stammer. Go into the kitchen to get a Diet Coke and throw the tape in the garbage. I'll say, "It's stupid. It's a stupid show. There's nothing to see."

I will be humiliated because I couldn't find the right words. I will feel that awful choked up feeling like I'm going to cry, but can't. Instead I'll count shades of pink. I'll go out to the living room and see my landlords just stare at me with their blank, blank eyes. Buddy will come closer to me. She'll get right up next to me, stare at me. She won't say anything. Thankfully. She'll crack a smile. She'll know it's bad and just let it go.

The next day I'll get up early to go for my run along the beach. Actually, I'll get up and act like I'm going for a run but in truth I'll walk down to the Rose Cafe in my jogging gear and order a mocha and a croissant. I'll sit down on one of the stools at one of the little round tables and look around. There will be a lot of women sitting alone, all dolled-up at 6:00 a.m. I'll figure they're actresses waiting to be discovered. Or models. They'll all have that anorexic look. I'll dump a packet of sugar in my mocha and stir it around. And that's when Buddy will walk in.

She will walk over and say, "A croissant too? Fancy today, huh?" I will look at her and pause. I will say, "What do you see in me? I mean really, I'm a wreck." She will smile and put her stuff down at my table. She'll go over and get a latte and a bagel with cream cheese. Normal breakfast stuff. She'll sit down and I'll look down at my feet dangling beneath me. I'll be too short to reach the floor. I'll instantly compare Buddy to my ex–imaginary lover. She will have a profile that stands out, but that may be the glasses. And I will like it that she gets me. Buddy will understand that I like all the things that go into sandwiches but not actual sandwiches and guacamole but not avacados. And I will look at Buddy and know what she's thinking. It will be like some extraterrestrial mind lock, where I can just feel the things she's feeling. Like that morning, I will just feel all the gentleness between us. It will remind me of rain in June. The scent and everything.

I'll take a sip of my mocha and ask her what review she's working on now. She will reach into her bag and pull out the *Los Angeles Times*. She'll say, "Speaking of my work, guess what just came out?" I will say, "I can't see it. Not after the Barbara Wa-was fiasco." I'll say, "I think this whole PR thing is out of control." Buddy will laugh. She'll say, "Okay, I'll put it away for now, but you know that you're reading it." And I'll say, "I know, of course, it's your work." And Buddy will say, "Thank you, but really, there's nothing to fear."

So I'll grab the paper out of her hands and read it all right there from start to finish. It will be an entire page and the title will read: "All the Pink You Can Eat."

Buddy will write not so much about pink as she does about me, the author. She will talk about her first review of me in college, how she panned me back then. She will say in order for art to mature, the artist must first mature. She will talk about my hiding, my lies, and my parents. And at first I will cringe, at first I will be terrified that my lies and deceit will be printed in the *Los Angeles Times,* but then I will see she is doing it for a reason. That my art, like my self, has evolved. She will say things like, "Although the writer is just entering this thing called adulthood, perhaps a bit late, you can see that her little pink book is her first real step, it is solid with a grace and humility that is much like the writer herself." And I will like that a lot. I will not be embarrassed by my need to be loved.

I will like it that despite all my blunders I can still be said to have a bit of grace. I will think that I need a lot more than I have, but in that moment I will look at Buddy Holly and know that whatever bit of grace there is in the world, it is not my own. That the thing she calls "grace" is something that comes from outside us, something that perhaps will have brought us together.

When the book I will write comes out, and I am in Chicago in my old apartment, I will get down on my knees and fish under my bed. I will pull out my brown bag of rejections and look at them. One by one. I will figure there are about thirty of my favorites still in there. I will pull one rejection after the other from the bag and look at the stamped dates and my name. The envelopes will be so old they're all yellowed. I will kiss each and every one and then slide the bag back under the bed. Let them all rest together.

The movie of my little pink book will be the big hit the Henrys have prayed for. At the opening all the hot stars will come. The who's who of hot. Even the actors who didn't get the parts they wanted will come. They will all be there preening. Buddy and I will walk the red carpet hand in hand and some entertainment show host will push a microphone in my face. They will say, "So how was it with Spielberg? What was the experience like?" And Buddy will squeeze my hand, as if to say, "Yes, this is real, it's okay, just talk slowly. Hold your head up." And I will. I will say it was wonderful that Mr. Spielberg is a dream. And then one of the stars will arrive and all the press will hurry after her.

At the premiere I will not be terribly important. I will be something of an afterthought. But in truth I will be happier that way and Buddy will just hold my hand. I will lean into Buddy and say it feels so strange that it's so out of my hands. I will say I feel a sort of loss but can't explain it. And Buddy will just weave her arm through mine. She will not say anything at all. We will walk into the movie theater together, my head leaning on her shoulder as we go. I will hope that my parents will be watching their TV in Chicago. I will hope they are nestled together with a blanket over their legs watching TV and smiling. I will hope that my parents will see the interview and how happy Buddy and I look together at the premiere of the movie of the book I will write.

By the book's fourth print run the publisher will call me up and ask if I can write a sequel. "This time," they'll say, "it'll be the little black book, you know, something dramatic. Something hot. Racy." I will be walking along the boardwalk in Venice, holding my cell phone up to my right ear, trying to plug my left ear by cupping it with my left hand. The Rollerblading electric guitar player will be following me down the boardwalk. I will listen as the publisher in New York lists all the possible colors and runs ideas past me for the next cover.

I won't say anything at all. I will think briefly about Spielberg and the Henrys and the set. Then I'll shift to Buddy, who will be waiting for me in our new two-bedroom home, and I will turn my head toward the ocean, smell the salt in the wind.

I can just see it.

ABOUT THE AUTHOR

Jennifer Harris's poetry has been published in several national magazines, including *New York Quarterly, Fish Stories, Art Times, Swerve,* and the anthology *Power Lines*. Her poetry is also forthcoming in the *Harrington Lesbian Literary Quarterly*. She founded and directed a three-year reading series at The Art Institute of Chicago, and during that same time founded and edited a small literary magazine called *JackLeg Press*. Jennifer is a past finalist in FourWay Books national book contest, and she was recognized by The Poetry Center of Chicago in their Emerging Young Poets Series. For the past five years, Jennifer has spent much of her free time helping the Tibetan monks from Drepung Gomang Monastery and was the 2005 director of their United States tour. She attended the University of Arizona as an undergraduate and completed her MFA in writing at the School of the Art Institute of Chicago.

HARRINGTON PARK PRESS®
Alice Street Editions™
Judith P. Stelboum
Editor in Chief

An Inexpressible State of Grace by Cameron Abbott

Minus One: A Twelve-Step Journey by Bridget Bufford

Girls with Hammers by Cynn Chadwick

Rosemary and Juliet by Judy MacLean

An Emergence of Green by Katherine V. Forrest

Descanso: A Soul Journey by Cynthia Tyler

Blood Sisters: A Novel of an Epic Friendship by Mary Jacobsen

Women of Mystery: An Anthology edited by Katherine V. Forrest

Glamour Girls: Femme/Femme Erotica by Rachel Kramer Bussel

The Meadowlark Sings by Helen R. Schwartz

Blown Away by Perry Wynn

Shadow Work by Cynthia Tyler

Hard Road, Easy Riding: Lesbian Biker Erotica edited by Sacchi Green and Rakelle Valencia

The Choice by Maria V. Ciletti

Pink by Jennifer Harris

Order a copy of this book with this form or online at:
http://www.haworthpress.com/store/product.asp?sku=5768

PINK

_____in softbound at $10.95 (ISBN-13: 978-1-56023-629-0; ISBN-10: 1-56023-629-9)

161 pages

Or order online and use special offer code HEC25 in the shopping cart.

COST OF BOOKS_____

POSTAGE & HANDLING_____
*(US: $4.00 for first book & $1.50
for each additional book)*
*(Outside US: $5.00 for first book
& $2.00 for each additional book)*

SUBTOTAL_____

IN CANADA: ADD 6% GST_____

STATE TAX_____
*(NJ, NY, OH, MN, CA, IL, IN, PA, & SD
residents, add appropriate local sales tax)*

FINAL TOTAL_____
*(If paying in Canadian funds,
convert using the current
exchange rate, UNESCO
coupons welcome)*

☐ **BILL ME LATER:** (Bill-me option is good on
US/Canada/Mexico orders only; not good to
jobbers, wholesalers, or subscription agencies.)

☐ Check here if billing address is different from
shipping address and attach purchase order and
billing address information.

Signature_____

☐ **PAYMENT ENCLOSED: $_____**

☐ **PLEASE CHARGE TO MY CREDIT CARD.**

☐ Visa ☐ MasterCard ☐ AmEx ☐ Discover
☐ Diner's Club ☐ Eurocard ☐ JCB

Account #_____

Exp. Date_____

Signature_____

Prices in US dollars and subject to change without notice.

NAME_____

INSTITUTION_____

ADDRESS_____

CITY_____

STATE/ZIP_____

COUNTRY_____ COUNTY (NY residents only)_____

TEL_____ FAX_____

E-MAIL_____

May we use your e-mail address for confirmations and other types of information?   ☐ Yes ☐ No
We appreciate receiving your e-mail address and fax number. Haworth would like to e-mail or fax special
discount offers to you, as a preferred customer. **We will never share, rent, or exchange your e-mail address
or fax number.** We regard such actions as an invasion of your privacy.

Order From Your Local Bookstore or Directly From

The Haworth Press, Inc.
10 Alice Street, Binghamton, New York 13904-1580 • USA
TELEPHONE: 1-800-HAWORTH (1-800-429-6784) / Outside US/Canada: (607) 722-5857
FAX: 1-800-895-0582 / Outside US/Canada: (607) 771-0012
E-mail to: orders@haworthpress.com

For orders outside US and Canada, you may wish to order through your local
sales representative, distributor, or bookseller.
For information, see http://haworthpress.com/distributors

(Discounts are available for individual orders in US and Canada only, not booksellers/distributors.)

PLEASE PHOTOCOPY THIS FORM FOR YOUR PERSONAL USE.
http://www.HaworthPress.com   BOF06

Dear Customer:

Please fill out & return this form to receive special deals & publishing opportunities for you! These include:
- availability of new books in your local bookstore or online
- one-time prepublication discounts
- free or heavily discounted related titles
- free samples of related Haworth Press periodicals
- publishing opportunities in our periodicals or Book Division

❑ OK! Please keep me on your regular mailing list and/or e-mailing list for new announcements!

Name _____

Address _____

STAPLE OR TAPE YOUR BUSINESS CARD HERE!

_____

*E-mail address _____

*Your e-mail address will never be rented, shared, exchanged, sold, or divested. You may "opt-out" at any time. May we use your e-mail address for confirmations and other types of information? ❑ Yes ❑ No

Special needs:
Describe below any special information you would like:
- Forthcoming professional/textbooks
- New popular books
- Publishing opportunities in academic periodicals
- Free samples of periodicals in my area(s)

Special needs/Special areas of interest:

_____

_____

_____

_____

Please contact me as soon as possible. I have a special requirement/project:

_____

_____

_____

The Haworth Press Inc.

PLEASE COMPLETE THE FORM ABOVE AND MAIL TO:
Donna Barnes, Marketing Dept., The Haworth Press, Inc.
10 Alice Street, Binghamton, NY 13904–1580 USA
Tel: 1–800–429–6784 • Outside US/Canada Tel: (607) 722–5857
Fax: 1–800–895–0582 • Outside US/Canada Fax: (607) 771–0012
E-mail: orders@HaworthPress.com

GBIC06

Visit our Web site: www.HaworthPress.com